Also by Jackie L. Smith

The Customs Conspiracy

Brynn Thornwick: Guardian of the Crimson Crown

Atlas Drummond: Fragments of Deceit

Colby Utterback: Finding His Place

The Last Whisper of Innocence

The Fractured Path to Emerald Vale Echoes of Betrayal

Hank Blankenship And The Longest Fall

Hank Blankenship And

The

Longest Fall

154 Years From Home

by

Jackie L. Smith

Copyright

Published by: Jackie L. Smith

Cover Design by: Jessica Stacey

First Edition

ISBN: 979-8-9959280-6-5 (paperback)

Printed and Published in the United States of America

Dedication

For Chester and Hazel — and for every kid who ever looked at the sky and wondered what was on the other side.

Epigraph

"The West is not a place. It's a time of day. It's a way of looking at things." — Louis L'Amour

Table of Contents

Author's Note

This novel is a work of fiction. While Buffalo, Wyoming, and Johnson County are real places with rich and fascinating histories, the characters and events in this story are entirely imaginary. No character is based on any real person, living or dead.

The historical setting of 1870 Wyoming Territory has been researched for accuracy, but certain details have been adjusted to serve the story. In 1870, the town of Buffalo did not yet exist — it was founded in 1879. The area along Clear Creek at the foot of the Bighorn Mountains was open range, home to scattered settlers and the very beginnings of Wyoming's cattle ranching industry.

Readers interested in the real history of Buffalo and Johnson County are encouraged to visit the Jim Gatchell Memorial Museum in Buffalo and the Hoof prints of the Past Museum in Kaycee, Wyoming.

Skydiving is an exhilarating but inherently dangerous activity. The skydiving club depicted in this novel follows established safety protocols. Anyone interested in skydiving should seek certified instruction through the United States Parachute Association (USPA).

CHAPTER 1: The Cowboy in Sneakers

The alarm went off at five in the morning, which was late by Henry (Hank) Blankenship's standards.

Most days he was up by four-thirty, dressed and downstairs before the coffee finished brewing, boots on and hat in hand by the time his father came through the kitchen. But this was a Friday in May, the last Friday before his final week of high school, and Hank had allowed himself the luxury of an extra thirty minutes in bed. He'd regret it later — there were always more chores than time — but right now, lying in the dark with the Bighorn Mountains invisible beyond his window, thirty minutes felt like a gift.

The alarm was his phone, propped on the nightstand beside a dog-eared copy of "Lonesome Dove" that he'd read four times. His room was a catalog of who he was — rodeo posters on the walls, a shelf of western history books, a pair of spurs his grandfather had left him, a framed photo of his first calf that he'd helped deliver when he was nine. On the floor by the door, exactly where he'd left them last night, sat his cowboy boots. Brown leather, worn at the heels, scuffed from three years of daily use. He owned sneakers — one pair, for skydiving — but he couldn't remember the last time he'd worn them for anything else.

Hank swung his legs out of bed, pulled on jeans and a

flannel shirt, and reached for the boots. They went on the way they always did — right foot first, then left, the leather warm and familiar. Then the hat. Straw Resistol, sweat-stained around the band, shaped the way he liked it after two years of daily wear. His friends at school said he looked like he'd stepped out of an old photograph. His buddy Travis said he should have been born in a prior century. Hank took it as a compliment every time.

He went downstairs. The house was a two-story ranch house on forty acres east of town — not big, not fancy, but solid the way things built by Chester Blankenship tended to be solid. Chester didn't believe in anything that couldn't survive a Wyoming winter, and that philosophy applied to houses, fences, and sons.

The kitchen light was already on. His mother stood at the stove with a spatula in one hand and a coffee mug in the other, managing both with the effortless coordination of a woman who'd been making breakfast for her family every morning for as long as Hank could remember.

"Morning, baby," Hazel said without turning around. She always knew who was coming down the stairs by the sound of their footsteps. Hank was steady and even. Sanger was heavy and fast. Jules sounded like a small herd of buffalo, which was ironic given they lived in a town named after one.

"Morning, Mom," Hank said. He poured himself coffee — black, no sugar, the way Chester drank it and the way Hank had started drinking it at fifteen because that's what ranch men did. "Dad out already?"

"Since four-thirty," Hazel said. "Number forty-seven is calving and he wanted to check on her before he fed the rest."

Number forty-seven was a four-year-old Hereford that had given Chester trouble with her first calf last spring. Hank had been the one to stay up all night with her, talking to her through the fence rails while Chester worked, and when the calf finally came — sideways, because forty-seven did nothing the easy way — it was Hank's hands that guided it out. Chester had clapped him on the shoulder afterward and said, "You've got the touch, son." Four words. From Chester Blankenship, that was a speech.

"I'll go help him after I eat," Hank said.

"Sit down first," Hazel said. She set a plate on the table — eggs, bacon, biscuits, the kind of breakfast that fueled a man through five hours of ranch work before lunch. Hazel Blankenship cooked like she did everything else — thoroughly, generously, and without accepting the possibility of failure. She ran a western clothing store on Main Street called Hazel's Outpost, and she ran her kitchen with the same combination of warmth and authority. You could argue with Hazel about politics or weather or the price of feed corn, but you did not argue about meals. Meals happened on time, at the table, and you ate what was put in front of you.

Hank sat and ate. The kitchen was warm, the coffee was strong, and through the window he could see the first light hitting the Bighorns — that pale gold that happened in May when the sun cleared the horizon and found the snow still clinging to the peaks. Buffalo, Wyoming, was a town of forty-six hundred people in Johnson County, and Hank had lived here all seventeen years of his life. He knew every street, every store, every ranch road within twenty miles. He knew the history — the Bozeman Trail, Fort Phil Kearny, the Johnson County War of 1892, the cattle barons and the homesteaders, Butch Cassidy hiding out at Hole-in-the-Wall. He'd been to the Jim Gatchell Museum so many times the staff knew him by name. He'd sat in the Occidental Hotel and imagined Owen Wister writing "The Virginian" at a table in the corner.

Buffalo was in his blood. The land, the mountains, the history, the cattle. This was where he belonged, and after graduation next week, he was staying. No college, no city, no leaving. Chester needed help with the ranch, and Hank wanted to give it. Sixty-five head of cattle didn't manage themselves, and Chester wasn't getting younger. The plan was simple — work the ranch, build the herd, eventually take over when Chester was ready to slow down. It was the life

Hank wanted and the life Chester had lived and the life his grandfather had lived before that. Three generations of Blankenships on Wyoming soil.

Sanger came downstairs at five-thirty. Fifteen, already broad in the shoulders, with the same dark hair and serious expression that all the Blankenship men shared. He was quieter than Hank — not shy, just careful with his words. He sat down and ate without talking, which was normal for Sanger before six in the morning.

Jules arrived at five-forty-five. Twelve, skinny, loud, the opposite of Sanger in every way. Jules entered rooms the way weather entered valleys — suddenly and with noise.

"Is there bacon?" Jules asked before he was fully through the doorway.

"There's always bacon," Hazel said. "Sit down."

"Hank, are you jumping tomorrow?" Jules asked. He grabbed three pieces of bacon before his plate was even on the table. "Can I come watch?"

"It's a formation jump," Hank said. "Six of us, all together. You can come if Mom says it's okay."

"Mom?" Jules turned to Hazel with the expression of a twelve-year-old who had already calculated the odds of success and found them favorable.

"We'll see," Hazel said. Which in Hazel's language

meant yes, but she wasn't going to admit it before six in the morning.

"That means yes," Jules said to Hank.

"That means we'll see," Hazel said. "Eat your breakfast."

The phone rang. Hazel looked at the screen, sighed, and answered.

"Good morning, Tammy," Hazel said. Her voice shifted into the particular register she reserved for her sisters — patient, warm, and prepared for whatever unsolicited advice was coming. "No, the boys aren't up yet — well, they are now. Yes, Hank is jumping tomorrow. No, I'm not worried. Yes, Chester is fine. No, I don't think Sanger needs a haircut."

Hank and Sanger exchanged a look. Aunt Tammy called every morning — sometimes before six, always with opinions. She lived in Sheridan, forty-five minutes north, and managed her sister's life with the dedication of a woman who had no children of her own and had therefore adopted Hazel's. Aunt Gylness was the same, except she lived in Casper and called in the evenings instead of the mornings, and her specialty was financial advice that nobody had asked for.

Hazel loved both her sisters without reservation. She

also had a limit on how much advice she could absorb before breakfast, and Tammy was testing it.

"Tammy, I need to go," Hazel said. "Chester's out with a calving cow and the boys still have chores before school. I'll call you tonight. Yes. I promise. Love you too. Bye."

She hung up and looked at her sons. "Your aunt says hello," Hazel said.

"Your aunt says we need haircuts," Sanger said without looking up from his eggs.

"Your aunt means well," Hazel said. "Eat."

Hank finished his plate, put it in the sink, and headed for the door. The morning was cool — May in Wyoming meant fifties at dawn, sometimes colder, the kind of air that smelled like sage and snowmelt and possibility. He walked to the barn where Chester was already working, his father's silhouette visible through the open doors against the early light.

Chester Blankenship was fifty-two, lean, weathered, and built from the same material as the fenceposts he drove into the ground every spring. He spoke in short sentences and long silences, and he taught his sons the way the land had taught him — by doing, by showing, by letting them fail small so they wouldn't fail big. He'd been ranching this land for twenty-five years, and before that his father had ranched it for thirty. The Blankenship ranch wasn't big by Wyoming standards — sixty-five head of mixed Hereford and Angus, forty acres owned and another two hundred leased for grazing. But it was theirs, and Chester maintained it with a pride that had nothing to do with money and everything to do with legacy.

"How's forty-seven?" Hank asked.

"Close," Chester said. He was leaning on the fence rail, watching the pregnant cow with the practiced patience of a man who'd been through this hundreds of times. "Maybe tonight. Maybe tomorrow. She's taking her time."

"She always takes her time," Hank said.

"She's particular," Chester said. "Like your mother."

Hank smiled. It was the closest Chester came to humor before seven in the morning.

They worked together for an hour — feeding, checking water, moving two yearlings to a different pasture, mending a section of fence that had come loose in last week's wind. Hank worked without being told what to do, because Chester had taught him the rhythm of a ranch the way other fathers taught their sons to ride a bike. You learned it once and it stayed in your body forever.

At seven, Hank cleaned up and drove to school. Buffalo High School was a low brick building on the east side of town that served every teenager in Johnson County, which wasn't many. Hank's graduating class had sixty-three students. He knew all of them. He'd known most of them since kindergarten.

He parked his truck — a 2009 Ford F-150 that Chester had given him for his sixteenth birthday, already old when he got it, now older and more dented but still running because Blankenships didn't throw things away that still worked. He walked in wearing what he always wore — jeans, boots, flannel shirt, the Resistol hat that he took off inside buildings because his mother had raised him right.

"Hey cowboy," said a voice from behind him. Travis Mackie, his closest friend at school, falling into step beside him. "You ready for tomorrow?"

"Born ready," Hank said.

"You're born a hundred years too late is what you are," Travis said. He looked at Hank's boots, his hat in his hand, the belt buckle he'd won at a junior rodeo three years ago. "When are you going to dress like a normal person?"

"When normal people start dressing better," Hank said.

Travis laughed. He was one of the five other members of the skydiving club who'd be jumping with Hank tomorrow — the Buffalo Sky Devils, which was an ambitious name for six teenagers who jumped out of a rented Cessna on weekends. The club had been Hank's idea. He'd gotten his first tandem jump for his fifteenth birthday — Chester's gift, the most expensive thing his father had ever bought him — and from the moment the chute opened and the Bighorns spread out below him like a painting, Hank was hooked.

The club met after school on Fridays to plan. Today's meeting was in the cafeteria at three-thirty — the five other members plus Hank, going over tomorrow's formation jump. Six divers, all exiting the Cessna within seconds of each other, forming up in freefall before deploying chutes. They'd done individual jumps and pairs, but this was their first full-team formation. The club had been practicing the sequence on the ground for weeks — body positions, spacing, hand signals.

Hank made it through the school day the way he always did — paying enough attention to maintain his B average, which was the club's requirement for membership, and spending the rest of his mental energy on cattle and sky. He'd never been a great student, but he wasn't a bad one either. He did the work because the work needed doing, the same way he mucked stalls and mended fences. Not because he loved it, but because discipline was something Chester had built into him the way you build a foundation into a house — first, and strong, and non-negotiable.

The meeting went well. The formation was planned. The jump time was set — ten in the morning, weather permitting. The pilot was confirmed. The landing zone was a flat pasture two miles south of town that a rancher let them use in exchange for the club helping with his fence line twice a year. Hank had organized that deal himself, because maintaining the club meant maintaining relationships, and maintaining relationships meant doing work for people who helped you. Chester had taught him that too.

After the meeting, Hank drove home. The sun was dropping toward the Bighorns, painting the sky in shades of orange and gold that happened nowhere else on earth the way they happened in Wyoming. He rolled down the truck window and let the air hit his face — cool, clean, carrying the smell of grass and distance.

Tomorrow he would jump. Six divers, one formation, the sky over Buffalo opening beneath them like a promise. He'd been thinking about it all week — the rush of freefall, the discipline of the formation, the moment when the chute opens and the world goes quiet and you float above everything, seeing the land the way eagles see it.

But tonight there were cattle to check and a calving cow to watch and dinner to eat at a table with his family and a phone call from Aunt Gylness to endure and homework to finish and boots to clean and a hat to hang on the hook by the door where it had hung every night of his life.

He pulled into the driveway. The house was lit up, warm against the cooling evening. Through the kitchen window, he could see Hazel at the stove. Through the barn door, he could see Chester's shadow moving among the animals. Somewhere inside, Sanger was doing homework quietly and Jules was doing homework loudly and the Blankenship family was being exactly what it had always been.

Home.

Hank parked the truck, put on his hat, and walked toward the barn to help his father. The Bighorns rose behind the house, enormous and patient, the same mountains that had watched over this valley for millions of years and would watch over it for millions more.

Tomorrow, he would jump.

He didn't know it would be the last ordinary evening of his life. He didn't know that the sky he loved — the sky he jumped into every chance he got, the sky that made him feel more alive than anything on the ground — was about to take him somewhere no parachute could bring him back from.

He didn't know any of that yet. He just knew it was Friday in May in Buffalo, Wyoming, and there were cattle to feed and a family to love and a jump to look forward to.

That was enough. It had always been enough.

CHAPTER 2: The Jump

Saturday morning, Hank was up at four-thirty. No extra thirty minutes today. The jump was at ten, but cattle didn't care about skydiving schedules, and Chester expected his sons to do their work before they did anything else.

The kitchen was dark when Hank came downstairs. Hazel wasn't up yet — Saturday was her one day to sleep past five, and the family respected it with the reverence that sacred things deserved. Hank made coffee, poured a mug for himself and a second one for Chester, and carried both to the barn.

Chester was already there. Of course he was. Hank had never once in seventeen years beaten his father to the barn. Chester took the coffee without a word, sipped it, and nodded toward the east pasture.

"Forty-seven calved at midnight," Chester said. "Bull calf. Both doing fine."

"I missed it?" Hank said.

"You needed sleep," Chester said. "Big day today."

That was as close as Chester Blankenship would come to acknowledging that his son was about to jump out of an airplane at ten thousand feet. Chester didn't fully understand skydiving. He understood horses, cattle, fences, weather, and the ground beneath his boots. The sky was something he looked at to predict rain, not something he fell through on purpose. But he'd bought Hank that first tandem jump at fifteen because his son had asked for it with the same quiet certainty he'd shown when he said he wanted to ranch instead of going to college. Chester recognized conviction when he saw it. He didn't have to understand it to respect it.

They worked for two hours. Fed the herd, checked the new calf — a strong little bull that had his mother's stubbornness and was already trying to stand — hauled water to the far trough, and walked the fence line along the north pasture. Sanger joined them at six, silent and efficient, taking his section of the work without being assigned it. Jules stumbled out at six-thirty, complaining about the cold, and was put to work stacking hay bales in the barn.

At seven-thirty, Hank cleaned up, changed into his jump gear, and came downstairs to find Hazel in the kitchen. She'd gotten up after all — couldn't stay in bed on a morning her oldest was jumping, even if she'd never say that was the reason.

"Breakfast is on the table," Hazel said. Eggs, bacon, biscuits. The same meal as yesterday. The same meal as every day. Consistency was Hazel's love language.

"Thanks, Mom," Hank said. He sat and ate. His jump bag was by the front door — suit, helmet, goggles, gloves, the sneakers he only wore for this. Everything else about Hank was cowboy. The sneakers were the one concession to a hobby that didn't exist in the century he should have been born in.

"Be careful up there," Hazel said. She said it every time he jumped. Not with worry — with the calm authority of a mother who expected her instructions to be followed.

"Always am," Hank said.

"And be home for dinner," Hazel said. "I'm making pot roast."

"Yes ma'am," Hank said.

Jules appeared in the kitchen doorway, still wearing hay dust. "Mom said I could come watch," Jules said.

"Mom said we'd see," Hazel said.

"That was yesterday," Jules said. "Today it's a yes. Right?"

Hazel looked at Jules. Jules looked at Hazel. The negotiation lasted three seconds.

"You ride with Hank," Hazel said. "You stay behind the fence at the landing zone. You don't touch any equipment. And you wear sunscreen."

"Deal," Jules said.

"I want to come too," Sanger said from the hallway.

He'd come in from chores and was standing in the doorway with his boots still on, which Hazel would normally comment on, but she let it go because it was a Saturday and her boys wanted to be together.

"Fine," Hazel said. "All three of you. Hank's in charge."

"Hank's always in charge," Jules said.

"That's because Hank doesn't argue with me before seven in the morning," Hazel said.

Chester came through the back door, boots muddy, hat in hand. He looked at Hank in his jump gear — the suit that didn't belong on a ranch, the bag of equipment that had nothing to do with cattle — and for a moment something crossed his face. Not disapproval. Something closer to wonder. The recognition that his eldest son contained a piece that didn't come from Chester or the ranch or three generations of Blankenship dirt. A piece that belonged to the sky.

"Good luck today," Chester said.

"Thanks, Dad," Hank said.

"Watch the wind at altitude," Chester said. "It was gusting last night. Might still be up there."

"I'll watch it," Hank said.

Chester nodded. Put his hat back on. Went back outside. The conversation was over, but what it contained — the luck, the practical advice, the permission to go do the thing that made no sense to a man whose life was measured in fenceposts and calving seasons — was more than enough.

Hank loaded his brothers into the truck at eight-thirty. The drive to the landing zone took fifteen minutes — south on the highway, then east on a ranch road that turned to dirt after the first gate. The pasture was flat and open, ringed by fence, with the Bighorns rising to the west and the rolling grassland stretching east toward the Powder River Basin. The rented Cessna was already there, parked on a strip of hard ground that served as a runway. The pilot — a retired crop duster named Earl who flew for the club on weekends — was doing his preflight check.

The other five club members were gathered by the plane, already in their gear. Hank parked the truck, told Jules and Sanger to stay behind the fence, and walked over with his bag.

"There he is," one of the guys said. "The cowboy. Ready to ride the sky?"

"Born ready," Hank said. The same thing he'd said to Travis yesterday. The same thing he said every time. It wasn't bravado. It was the simple truth of a boy who'd found the one thing in the modern world that felt as real as ranching.

They went through the plan one more time. Six divers, exiting the Cessna at ten thousand feet within seconds of each other. Freefall in a star formation — each diver taking a position, holding it for ten seconds, then breaking apart and deploying chutes individually. They'd practiced the positions on the ground a dozen times. The formation was simple by competitive standards, but it was the most complex thing the Buffalo Sky Devils had attempted, and the energy among the group was equal parts excitement and focus.

"Jump order," Hank said. He'd planned it based on weight and experience. The heaviest jumpers went first because they fell faster and needed more time to get into position. Hank, the most experienced, went last so he could track the formation from above and adjust his approach. "I'm tail. Everybody else, same order we practiced. Exit clean, get stable, find your position. I'll come in from above and close the star. Ten-second hold, then break and deploy. Questions?"

No questions. They'd gone over this a dozen times. Everybody knew their job.

Earl finished his checks and waved them over. "Weather's good," Earl said. "Wind at altitude is eight knots from the northwest. Nothing you can't handle. I'll take you up to ten thousand and circle once so you can check the landing zone from up top. Then it's your show."

They loaded into the Cessna — six divers in a plane built for four passengers, which meant knees touching and elbows bumping and the particular closeness of people about to share something extraordinary. Earl taxied down the dirt strip, and the plane lifted off with the shuddering grace of a machine that was older than everyone in it except Earl himself.

Hank sat by the door. Below him, the landing zone shrank — the flat pasture, the fence, two small figures standing behind it that were Jules and Sanger watching their brother rise into the sky. Beyond the pasture, the town of Buffalo. Beyond the town, the Bighorn Mountains, still capped with snow, enormous and ancient. And beyond everything, the sky — blue and deep and endless, the color of possibility.

At ten thousand feet, Earl leveled off and circled. Hank looked down through the open door. The landing zone was visible — a green rectangle in a landscape of brown and gold. The wind sock at the edge of the field showed a steady breeze from the northwest, manageable. Conditions were good.

"Ready when you are," Earl called back.

Hank looked at his team. Five faces, goggles up,

waiting. The moment before a jump was always the same —
the pause between the decision and the act, the heartbeat
when the body said "don't do this" and the mind said "this is
exactly what you were made to do."

"Go," Hank said.

The first diver went out the door. Then the second.
Third. Fourth. Fifth. Each one dropping into the blue, falling
away from the plane, getting small. Hank watched them go,
counting seconds, waiting for his moment. Below him, five
bodies were spreading out, finding their positions, beginning
to form the star.

Hank stepped to the door. The wind grabbed at his
suit, cold and sharp at ten thousand feet. The Bighorns were
to his left, massive and white-topped. The Powder River
Basin stretched to his right, brown and rolling, endless.

He jumped.

The first second was always the best — the moment
when gravity took over and the plane disappeared above you
and there was nothing between you and the earth but ten
thousand feet of air. Freefall. The purest kind of freedom. No
engine, no wings, no machine. Just your body and the sky
and the ground coming up to meet you at a hundred and
twenty miles per hour.

Hank stabilized — arms out, legs spread, belly to the

earth. He looked down, scanning for the formation. Five divers below him, forming the star, each one visible against the patchwork of the land beneath them.

Except they weren't there.

Hank blinked. Looked again. The five divers who'd exited the plane seconds before him — his teammates, his friends, the people he'd planned this formation with for weeks — were gone. Not scattered, not off-position. Gone. The sky below him was empty.

And the ground was wrong.

The landing zone — the flat pasture with the fence and the wind sock and his brothers standing behind the wire — wasn't there. The town of Buffalo wasn't there. The highway wasn't there. The buildings and roads and power lines and everything that made the twenty-first century visible from ten thousand feet — none of it was there.

Below him was land. Open, endless, unmarked land. Grass and creek and mountains. The Bighorns were there — the same peaks, the same snow, the same ancient shape he'd seen from this altitude a dozen times. And Clear Creek was there — the silver thread winding through the valley, exactly where it always was.

But everything else was gone. No town. No roads. No fences. No buildings. Just the land as it might have looked before anyone built anything on it. Raw. Empty. Untouched.

Hank's altimeter read four thousand feet. He'd been falling and staring and not paying attention, which was the one thing you never did in freefall. He pulled his cord. The chute deployed — a sharp jolt as the canopy caught air and his descent went from a hundred and twenty miles per hour to fifteen. Silence rushed in. The wind dropped to a whisper. And Hank floated above a world he didn't recognize.

He steered toward the creek. When you didn't know where you were, you went to water — Earl had taught him that on his first jump. Water meant people, shelter, direction. The creek below him was Clear Creek, he was sure of it — the same curves, the same path through the valley, the same relationship to the mountains. But the banks were wild, overgrown, untouched by anything human except maybe a game trail.

He came in low over a meadow beside the creek. Tall grass, wildflowers, a flat stretch of ground that looked like it had never been walked on. He flared the chute, hit the ground running, and came to a stop in knee-high grass with the parachute billowing behind him like a strange white flag.

Hank stood in the meadow and looked around.

No landing zone. No fence. No wind sock. No Jules and Sanger behind the wire. No truck in the distance. No plane in the sky. No sound of traffic or machinery or anything that belonged to the world he'd jumped out of sixty seconds ago.

Silence. The kind of silence that didn't exist in 2024 — complete, unbroken, so deep that Hank could hear his own heartbeat and the creek running and a bird somewhere in the cottonwoods and nothing else. No engine. No radio. No hum of electricity. Nothing.

He pulled off his helmet. The air hit his face — the same May air, the same temperature, the same smell of sage and grass. But cleaner somehow. Sharper. Like air that had never been breathed through a car exhaust or a furnace vent.

He looked down at himself. Jumpsuit. Helmet in his hand. Goggles around his neck. Sneakers on his feet. The parachute spread across the meadow behind him like something from another world.

Which, Hank was beginning to realize, it was.

He didn't know where he was. He didn't know when he was. He didn't know how a boy could jump out of a plane over Buffalo, Wyoming, in May of 2024 and land in a place where Buffalo didn't exist.

All he knew was that the Bighorns were in the right place and the creek was in the right place and the sky was in the right place. Everything else was wrong.

He gathered his chute, bundled it as best he could, and started walking toward the only structure he could see — a thin curl of smoke rising from somewhere upstream along the creek, barely visible against the blue sky.

Smoke meant fire. Fire meant people. People meant answers.

Hank put his helmet under his arm, slung the bundled parachute over his shoulder, and walked through the tall grass in his sneakers toward a world he didn't understand yet.

The Bighorns watched him go. The same mountains. The same valley. The same creek.

A different century.

CHAPTER 3: Joshua

The smoke was coming from a tin chimney pipe sticking out of the saddest excuse for a building Hank had ever seen.

It sat about two hundred yards upstream from where he'd landed, tucked into a stand of cottonwoods along the creek bank. It was a shack — no other word for it. Rough-cut timber walls, a roof that was half planks and half canvas, a door that hung on leather hinges, and a single window covered with something that might have been oiled paper. The whole structure leaned slightly to the east, as if it had been arguing with the wind for years and was slowly losing.

A horse was tied to a rail out front — a buckskin, old but well cared for, munching on grass that grew between the rail posts. A stack of firewood sat against one wall. A washbasin hung from a nail. And from inside the shack, Hank could hear someone talking.

Not to another person. To the horse. Or maybe to the coffee. Or maybe to nobody at all. The voice was low and steady and carried the kind of easy rhythm that belonged to a person who'd been having one-sided conversations for so long they'd forgotten they were alone.

Hank stopped twenty feet from the door. He was still

in his jumpsuit. Still carrying the bundled parachute. Still wearing sneakers. He looked like nothing that had ever walked along Clear Creek in any century, and he knew it.

The voice inside stopped. The door opened.

The man standing in the doorway was somewhere between ancient and eternal. He was short — maybe five-six — and built like a fencepost that had been whittled down by decades of weather. Bowlegged in a way that said he'd spent more of his life on a horse than off one. White hair under a hat so old and shapeless it looked like it had been sat on by the horse outside. Whiskers that hadn't seen a razor in a week, maybe two. Eyes the color of creek water — pale, clear, sharp.

He looked at Hank. Then at the jumpsuit. Then at the parachute. Then at the sneakers. Then back at Hank's face. His expression didn't change. Not surprise, not fear, not confusion. Just the steady evaluation of a man who'd seen a lot of strange things in sixty-four years and had learned not to waste energy being startled by any of them.

"Well," the old man said. "Ain't you somethin'."

"Sir, I —" Hank started.

"Hold on, hold on," the old man said. He held up one hand — gnarled, sun-darkened, the hand of a man who'd worked every day of his life. "Before you get to talkin', I got one question. You hungry?"

"I — yes sir," Hank said. "I am."

"Then come in and eat," the old man said. "Whatever else is goin' on with you and that —" He gestured at the parachute. "—that big ole bedsheet you're carryin', it can wait till you got food in your belly. A man thinks better when he ain't hungry. That's the first rule of bein' alive."

He turned and went inside. Hank stood in the May sunshine with his mouth open and his parachute over his shoulder and the Bighorn Mountains rising behind him, and followed a stranger into a shack because the stranger had offered him food and Hank didn't have a better plan.

The inside of the shack was one room. A cot against one wall, covered with a wool blanket. A wood stove — the source of the chimney smoke — with a coffee pot and a cast iron skillet on top. A rough table made from split logs, two stools, a shelf with a few tin plates and cups. Everything was worn, patched, repaired, and clean. Poor but proud. The home of a man who didn't have much but took care of what he had.

The old man poured coffee into a tin cup and set it in front of Hank. Then he scraped something from the skillet onto a plate — beans, some kind of flatbread, a strip of dried meat that could have been beef or deer or something else entirely.

"Eat," the old man said. He sat on the other stool and poured his own coffee. "Name's Joshua Bettington. Most folks call me Josh, but I ain't particular. Been livin' on this stretch of creek goin' on three years now. Retired, if you can call it that. Worked cattle down in Colorado Territory for twenty years before my back said it was done and my knees agreed with it."

Hank ate. The beans were plain, the bread was tough, and the meat tasted like salt and smoke. It was the best meal he'd ever had, because he was hungry and scared and sitting in a shack with a man who didn't seem bothered by the fact that a boy in strange clothes had just walked out of nowhere carrying a giant sheet of fabric.

"Thank you, sir," Hank said. "I'm Hank. Henry Blankenship. People call me Hank."

"Hank," Joshua repeated. He said it the way you'd taste something new — rolling it around, checking if it fit. "That's a good solid name. Where you from, Hank? And I'm askin' mainly because of that outfit you're wearin', which I ain't never seen the like of in all my born days."

This was the moment Hank had been dreading since his boots — his sneakers — hit the ground. What do you tell a man in what you're increasingly sure is the nineteenth century about where you came from?

"I'm from here," Hank said. "From this area. But I — I think something happened to me. I was in the sky. Falling.

And when I landed, everything was different."

"In the sky," Joshua said. He took a sip of coffee, considering this. "Fallin' from where?"

"From a — from a machine," Hank said. He knew the word "airplane" would mean nothing. "A flying machine. It goes up in the air and people can jump from it with this —" He pointed to the parachute bundle by the door. "— which opens up and slows you down so you land soft."

Joshua looked at the parachute. Then at Hank. Then at the ceiling of his shack, as if checking to make sure it was still there.

"A flyin' machine," Joshua said slowly. "That carries people up in the air. And then they jump out. On purpose."

"Yes sir," Hank said.

"And that bedsheet thing opens up and floats 'em down like a dandelion seed," Joshua said.

"That's pretty much exactly right," Hank said.

Joshua was quiet for a moment. He stared into his coffee cup with the expression of a man who was having a conversation with himself and wasn't sure who was winning.

"Son," Joshua said finally. "I don't know what a flyin'

machine is. I don't know why a person would jump out of one if they had one. And I sure as Sunday don't understand how a bedsheet keeps a man from bustin' his skull on the ground. But I've lived sixty-four years on this earth, and the one thing I've learned is that the world is bigger than what I've seen of it. So if you're tellin' me you fell out of the sky, I ain't gonna call you a liar. I'm just gonna say that's the damnedest thing I ever heard, and leave it at that."

Hank almost laughed. Not because it was funny — because Joshua's response was so practical, so unshakable, so completely without panic that it was the most reassuring thing anyone could have said.

"Mr. Bettington —" Hank started.

"Joshua," the old man said. "Or Josh. Mister Bettington was my daddy, and he's been dead twenty years."

"Joshua," Hank said. "What year is it?"

Joshua looked at him the way you'd look at someone who'd asked what color the sky was. "It's 1870, son. May of 1870. You don't know what year it is?"

The number hit Hank like a physical blow. 1870. He'd known it — had been circling around it since the moment he looked down from four thousand feet and saw no town, no roads, no modern anything. But hearing it spoken out loud by a man sitting three feet away made it real in a way that his own suspicion hadn't.

He was in 1870. One hundred and fifty-four years before the morning he'd eaten breakfast in his mother's kitchen and helped his father check a calving cow and driven his brothers to a landing zone where they were probably still standing behind a fence, wondering why their brother hadn't come down from the sky.

"Son?" Joshua's voice cut through the noise in Hank's head. "You look like you seen a ghost. Or maybe like you are one."

"I'm not a ghost," Hank said. His voice came out steadier than he expected. "But I think I'm very far from home."

"Where's home?" Joshua asked.

Hank looked out the shack's single window — the oiled paper letting in light but not a clear view. Through the door, he could see the creek. Clear Creek. The same creek that ran through the Buffalo he knew, the Buffalo where his family lived, the Buffalo that wouldn't exist for another nine years.

"Right here," Hank said. "Home is right here. But not yet."

Joshua studied him for a long time. The old man's eyes were sharp despite his age — the eyes of someone who'd spent decades reading cattle and weather and men, and who'd learned that the truth usually showed up in the things people didn't say.

"You ain't crazy," Joshua said. It wasn't a question. "I've known crazy. Worked with a fella down in Colorado who thought he was Napoleon Bonaparte and tried to ride a bull into Denver. You ain't that kind of off. You're somethin' else."

"I'm something else," Hank agreed.

"All right then," Joshua said. He stood, took Hank's empty plate, and set it in the washbasin. "Here's what I know. You fell out of the sky. You're wearin' clothes I ain't never seen. You don't know what year it is. And you say you're from here but not yet, which don't make a lick of sense but you said it like you meant it. So here's what I'm gonna do. I'm gonna give you a place to sleep tonight. Tomorrow, we'll figure out what comes next. A man shouldn't have to figure out his whole life on an empty stomach and no sleep."

"You'd do that?" Hank asked. "You don't even know me."

"Son, I live alone in a shack on a creek in the middle of nowhere," Joshua said. "Nearest neighbor is Herman Thamon, and he's six miles east. Last person I talked to was a Crow Indian two weeks ago who traded me venison for coffee. I ain't exactly overflowed with company." He pointed to a spot on the floor beside the stove. "It ain't much, but it's warm and it's dry. I'll get you a blanket."

"Thank you," Hank said. The words felt thin —

inadequate for what Joshua was offering. Not just a floor to sleep on, but the willingness to take in a stranger who'd fallen from the sky wearing things that didn't exist yet, without asking for proof or explanation or anything except a name.

"Don't thank me," Joshua said. "Thank the Lord you landed near someone who was raised right. Half the men in this territory would've shot you for them sneakers, just on account of bein' confused by 'em."

He said "sneakers" like it was a word from a foreign language, which, Hank supposed, it was.

That afternoon, Joshua gave Hank a tour of his world — which was small in size but large in character. The shack, the creek, the horse, the patch of ground where he grew beans and kept a few chickens. The Bighorn Mountains rising to the west, still snow-capped, enormous. The open grassland stretching east and south, unbroken by any fence or road or building. Just land. More land than Hank had ever seen without a single mark of human habitation on it.

"This whole valley's open range," Joshua said. They

were walking along the creek, Joshua moving with the stiff, rolling gait of a man whose body had been shaped by a lifetime in the saddle. "Government land, free for the takin'. Couple of ranchers movin' in — Thamon's the biggest, got himself maybe a hundred fifty head and plans for more. Others comin' in from down south, bringin' cattle up from Texas and Colorado. It's gonna be somethin' eventually. Right now it's just grass and sky and a whole lot of nothin'."

"And Native Americans," Hank said. He knew the history — Sioux, Cheyenne, Arapaho. This was their land, had been for centuries. The forts along the Bozeman Trail had been abandoned two years ago after the Treaty of Fort Laramie. The area was supposed to be Indian territory now, but settlers were already moving in, and the tensions that would lead to the Great Sioux War of 1876 were building.

Joshua looked at him sideways. "You know about the Indians?" Joshua asked.

"Some," Hank said. Careful. He couldn't explain that he'd learned it from books and museums and a lifetime of living in a town built on the history Joshua was currently living through.

"They're around," Joshua said. "Crow mostly, in this stretch. Sioux further east. We leave each other be, mostly. I trade with 'em when they come by. Coffee for venison. Tobacco for hides. They ain't the problem some folks make 'em out to be, long as you show respect." He spat. "It's the white men you gotta watch. Fellas comin' in with big plans and no manners. Takin' land, shootin' at anything that moves, treatin' the territory like it's theirs by right. That's where the trouble's gonna come from, mark my words."

Hank said nothing. He knew Joshua was right. The trouble was coming — the Custer fight in '76, the wars, the reservations, the Johnson County War in '92. All of it was ahead, written in the history books that Hank had read in a world that hadn't happened yet.

They walked back to the shack as the sun dropped behind the Bighorns. The light turned gold, then orange, then the deep purple that happened in Wyoming when the day gave up and the night came in. Hank had seen a thousand sunsets over these mountains. This one looked the same as every other. And completely different.

Because in 2024, sunset meant dinner at Hazel's table. It meant checking on the cattle with Chester. It meant Jules being loud and Sanger being quiet and Aunt Gylness calling with advice nobody wanted. It meant home.

Here, sunset meant a tin plate of beans, a blanket on the floor of a shack, and the sound of a sixty-four-year-old man talking to his horse while he put it up for the night.

"You're thinkin' about home," Joshua said. He'd come back inside and was banking the stove for the night, moving with the deliberate efficiency of a man who'd done this exact sequence of actions ten thousand times.

"Yeah," Hank said.

"Folks there?" Joshua asked.

"My mom and dad," Hank said. "Two younger brothers. Jules and Sanger."

"Good names," Joshua said. "Strong names."

"My dad's a rancher," Hank said. "Sixty-five head. I was supposed to take over after I finished school."

"Rancher, huh?" Joshua's interest sharpened. "You know cattle?"

"I've been working cattle since I was nine," Hank said.

"Well now," Joshua said. He settled onto his cot, pulling the wool blanket over his legs. "That's the first thing you've told me that makes complete sense. A boy who knows cattle is a boy who can make his way anywhere. Even —" He waved his hand vaguely at the world outside. "—wherever and whenever this is for you."

Hank lay on the blanket Joshua had given him, on the floor beside the stove, in a shack on Clear Creek in the year 1870. The warmth from the stove soaked into his bones. The sound of the creek came through the walls — the same creek that ran through his town, his home, his century. And above him, through a gap in the roof planks, he could see a single star.

The same stars. The same mountains. The same creek. A different world.

He thought about Hazel. About the pot roast she'd

made for dinner tonight — or would make, or had made, 154 years from now. He thought about Chester checking on cow forty-seven and the new bull calf. About Jules and Sanger standing behind the fence at the landing zone, watching the sky, waiting for their brother to come down.

They were still waiting. Or they had waited and given up. Or they were calling the police, searching the fields, his mother crying, his father silent in the way Chester got silent when something was too big for words.

Hank closed his eyes and felt the homesickness settle into him like cold water filling a well. Deep, slow, complete. The kind of missing that lived in your chest and made breathing feel like work.

"Joshua?" Hank said.

"Yeah, son?" Joshua's voice was drowsy, already half asleep.

"Thank you," Hank said. "For taking me in. For not thinking I'm crazy."

"I didn't say I don't think you're crazy," Joshua said.

"I said I ain't gonna call you a liar. There's a difference." A pause. "But you're welcome. Ain't nobody should have to sleep outside when there's a roof available, even if the roof's got holes in it."

"Goodnight, Joshua," Hank said.

"Goodnight, Hank," Joshua said. "And son? Whatever happened to you — wherever you come from and however you got here — you're here now. That's all that matters in the mornin'. You're here now."

You're here now.

Hank lay in the dark and listened to the creek and the wind and the old man's breathing and the vast, enormous silence of a world that hadn't been filled with noise yet. And somewhere in that silence, between the fear and the homesickness and the impossibility of everything that had happened since he jumped out of a plane six hours ago, he felt something else.

Not peace — it was too soon for peace. But the small, stubborn seed of something that might grow into peace if he gave it time.

He was here now. In 1870. On Clear Creek. In a shack with an old cowboy who'd offered him food and a floor and the gift of not being called crazy.

Tomorrow he'd figure out the rest. Tomorrow he'd

think about how to survive in a world without electricity or medicine or his mother's cooking. Tomorrow he'd deal with the fact that he was 154 years from home with no way back.

But tonight, he was warm. He was fed. He wasn't alone.

And in 1870, that was enough.

CHAPTER 4: 1870

Hank woke to the smell of coffee and the sound of a horse that was unimpressed with the morning.

For three seconds, he didn't know where he was. The ceiling was wrong — too low, too rough, daylight coming through gaps in the planks. The bed was wrong — not a bed at all, a blanket on a hard floor. The sounds were wrong — no furnace, no hum of electricity, no Jules thundering down the stairs.

Then he remembered. The jump. The empty sky. The wrong ground. Joshua's shack. The tin cup of coffee and the flatbread and the old man who'd said "you're here now, son" like it was the most obvious thing in the world.

1870. He sat up. His body ached — the floor had done his back no favors, and muscles he didn't know he had were stiff from the jump and the walk and the tension of the strangest day of his life. Through the door, which Joshua had propped open with a rock, Hank could see the creek — Clear Creek, silver in the early light, running over stones that would still be there in 2024. The Bighorns rose behind it, snow-capped, enormous, exactly where they belonged.

The same mountains. The same creek. Everything else, gone.

Joshua was outside, talking to the buckskin horse while he poured grain into a wooden trough. The horse — which Hank now saw was older than he'd first thought, maybe fifteen, with a sway in her back and gray around her muzzle — ate with the deliberate pace of an animal that had stopped hurrying years ago.

"Mornin'," Joshua said when Hank came outside. "Coffee's on the stove. Help yourself. There's biscuits too, if you can call 'em that. I ain't much of a baker."

Hank poured coffee and ate a biscuit that was more like a rock with ambition. He stood in the doorway of the shack and looked at the world — the vast, open, unmarked world of 1870 Wyoming Territory. No roads. No fences except a small corral Joshua had built for the horse. No buildings except the shack. Just grass and sky and mountains and the creek, stretching in every direction without a single sign that human beings had done anything to it beyond build one sad little shelter and tie up one old horse.

"It's big," Hank said. It was the only word that fit.

"Biggest country I ever seen," Joshua said. "And I seen a fair amount. Colorado, Kansas, Nebraska, come up through the territories. Ain't nothin' like this valley though. Man could stand here and see fifty miles in every direction and not lay eyes on another living soul."

"That doesn't bother you?" Hank asked. "Being this alone?"

Joshua scratched the horse behind her ears. "Used to," Joshua said. "First year out here, I talked to the horse so much she started answerin' back. Or I thought she did. Might've been the wind." He grinned — a wide, gap-toothed grin that transformed his weathered face into something surprisingly warm. "You get used to it. The quiet, the space, the bein' alone. After twenty years of bunkhouses and cattle drives and other men's snorin', the quiet was a gift. Now I'd rather talk to Dolly here than any man alive."

"Dolly?" Hank said.

"The horse," Joshua said. "Named after a gal I knew in Denver. The horse is better lookin' and smells better too."

Hank almost smiled. Almost. But the homesickness was sitting in his chest like a stone, and smiling felt like a betrayal of everything he'd lost twenty-four hours ago.

"We need to get you out of them clothes," Joshua said. He looked at Hank's jumpsuit — the bright fabric, the zippers, the material that didn't exist in any century Joshua had lived through. "You walk around in that outfit and the first person who sees you is gonna think you're either a spirit or a lunatic. Either way, it don't end well for you."

"I don't have anything else," Hank said. "Everything I

own is 154 years from here."

"I got extras," Joshua said. "They ain't fancy and they ain't new, but they'll keep you dressed and keep folks from shootin' at you on account of your appearance."

He went inside and came back with a bundle — trousers, a cotton shirt, a leather vest, a hat that was newer than Joshua's but not by much. And boots. Real cowboy boots, worn at the heels, creased at the ankles, the leather dark with years of use.

"They were mine when I was younger and my feet was bigger," Joshua said. "Try 'em on."

Hank changed inside the shack. The trousers were loose but held up with a belt Joshua provided. The shirt was soft from a hundred washings. The vest smelled like leather and wood smoke. The hat fit better than he expected. And the boots — Hank pulled them on and felt something shift inside him. Not comfort exactly. Recognition. His feet knew this shape. His body knew this weight. He'd worn cowboy boots every day of his life since he was old enough to choose his own shoes. These weren't his boots, but they were boots, and in a world where nothing else was familiar, they were enough.

He looked down at himself. A boy from 2024 dressed like a man from 1870. The jumpsuit, the helmet, the goggles, the sneakers, the parachute — all of it bundled on the floor, artifacts from a world that wouldn't exist for over a century.

"We should hide my gear," Hank said. "If someone sees it —"

"Already thought of that," Joshua said. He knelt beside the cot and pried up two floorboards, revealing a shallow space between the floor and the dirt beneath the shack. "Put it under here. Ain't nobody gonna look under my floor. Ain't nobody gonna look under my anything, to be honest. I ain't exactly a high-value target for thieves."

Hank packed his gear into the space — jumpsuit folded tight, helmet wrapped in the chute fabric, sneakers tucked alongside. The parachute took the most room, even compressed. When everything was in, Joshua replaced the boards and set the cot back over them.

"There," Joshua said. "Far as the world knows, you're just a kid from back East who wandered in lookin' for work. That's a story folks around here will believe, because it happens regular enough. Young men come out to the territory all the time lookin' for a new start."

"A kid from back East," Hank said.

"You got a better story?" Joshua asked.

"Not one that anybody would believe," Hank said.

"Then back East it is," Joshua said. "Now — you told

me last night your daddy's a rancher. Sixty-five head. And you been workin' cattle since you was nine. That true?"

"That's true," Hank said.

"Show me," Joshua said.

They spent the morning walking Joshua's small piece of land. He didn't have cattle — couldn't afford them, couldn't work them alone with his bad back and worse knees. But the land along the creek was good grazing land, and Joshua knew enough about cattle to test Hank's knowledge with questions that got harder as the morning went on.

"What do you do when a cow won't take her calf?" Joshua asked.

"Depends on why," Hank said. "If she's a first-time mother, you give her time in a quiet pen with the calf. Skin-to-skin contact. If she's rejecting because of illness, you treat the illness first. If the calf is weak, you supplement with bottle feeding until it's strong enough to nurse. And you never force it — a cow that's pushed too hard will kick and you'll lose the calf."

Joshua stared at him. "Who taught you that?" Joshua asked.

"My dad," Hank said.

"Your daddy must be one hell of a cattleman," Joshua said.

"He is," Hank said. And the stone in his chest grew heavier because Chester was one hell of a cattleman 154 years from now, and right now he was probably standing in a pasture wondering where his oldest son had gone.

"What about grazin'?" Joshua asked. "You just let 'em eat where they want?"

"No," Hank said. "You rotate pastures. Move the herd every few weeks so the grass can recover. If you let cattle eat the same ground too long, they kill it. The roots die, the soil erodes, and next year you've got dust instead of pasture."

"Rotate pastures," Joshua repeated. He said it like he was tasting a new food. "I ain't never heard of such a thing. Every rancher I know just lets the cattle roam and hopes for the best."

"That works when you've got unlimited range," Hank said. "But when more ranchers come in and the range gets smaller, you need to manage it or you lose everything."

"More ranchers are comin'," Joshua said. "Herman Thamon was the first big one, but there's talk of others movin' up from Colorado and Texas. This valley's gonna fill up."

"It will," Hank said. He knew exactly how it would fill up — the cattle boom of the 1870s and '80s, the Johnson County War, the homesteaders, the fences. The whole history of Wyoming ranching was ahead of them, and Hank was the only person alive who knew how it ended.

"Son, you know more about cattle than men twice your age," Joshua said. "And you handle yourself like somebody who's been doin' this work for years, not months. I don't know where you come from — or when you come from, since you seem to think that matters — but I know this. You could make a living in this territory. A good one. If you're willin' to work."

"I'm willing," Hank said. "I've never been anything but willing to work."

"Then tomorrow we ride over to Thamon's place," Joshua said. "Six miles east. He's been lookin' for hands since spring. Most of the men who come through are drifters — they work a month and move on. A boy who knows cattle and ain't afraid to stay put? Thamon would pay good money for that."

"I don't have a horse," Hank said.

"You'll ride Dolly," Joshua said. "She's slow and she's opinionated, but she'll get you there. And Hank — wear the hat. Out here, a man without a hat is a man who don't know what he's doin'. First impression matters."

"Joshua," Hank said. "Why are you helping me? You don't know me. You don't know where I'm really from. I showed up out of nowhere in clothes you've never seen, told you a story that makes no sense, and you're giving me your clothes and your horse and helping me find work. Why?"

Joshua was quiet for a moment. He looked at the creek, at the mountains, at the big empty country that surrounded them.

"Because I was young once," Joshua said. "And I was alone once. And somebody helped me when they didn't have to. Old rancher down in Colorado, name of Pete Sweeney. I showed up at his place half starved and dumber than a fence post, and he gave me a meal and a job and taught me everything I know about cattle and about bein' a man. I never forgot that." He looked at Hank. "I ain't got children. Never married. Never had anybody to pass things along to. And then you fell out of the sky — don't ask me to explain that, because I can't — and you're standin' in my yard knowin' more about cattle than I learned in twenty years, and you got nowhere to go and nobody to help you." He shrugged. "Seemed like the Lord was bein' pretty clear about what He wanted me to do."

Hank felt something in his throat that wasn't homesickness. It was gratitude — deep, unexpected, the kind that comes when a stranger treats you like family for no reason other than the fact that it's the right thing to do.

"Thank you, Joshua," Hank said.

"Stop thankin' me," Joshua said. "Start learnin' how to saddle Dolly. She's particular about the cinch and she'll bite you if you do it wrong."

They spent the rest of the afternoon working around the shack — chopping wood, mending the chicken coop, hauling water from the creek. Hank worked the way Chester had taught him — steady, thorough, finishing each task before starting the next. Joshua watched him the way a man watches a horse he's thinking about buying — assessing the stride, the temperament, the willingness to do the work without being prodded.

"You'll do fine at Thamon's," Joshua said as the sun started its drop behind the Bighorns. "Just keep your mouth shut about flyin' machines and bedsheets and what year you think it really is. Out here, a man's judged by what he can do, not where he came from. You can do plenty."

That night, Hank lay on his blanket beside the stove and listened to the silence. The enormous, empty, 1870 silence that had no engines in it, no electricity, no television playing in the next room, no Jules yelling about something, no phone buzzing with a text from Travis asking if he'd practiced the formation.

He thought about his family. He didn't know how time worked between his world and this one — whether minutes were passing in 2024 or hours or days. But he knew his parents would be looking for him. The skydiving club, the police, maybe search and rescue. They'd be searching the landing zone, the fields, the roads. Looking everywhere except 154 years in the past.

Hazel would be in the kitchen. Not cooking — standing, probably, with the phone in her hand, waiting for it to ring. Chester would be outside, because Chester handled everything by moving, by working, by doing something physical because sitting still when your son was missing was impossible.

Jules would be scared. Sanger would be quiet. And Aunt Tammy and Aunt Gylness would both be there, for once not giving advice, just being present, because even meddling sisters knew when to stop talking and start holding.

Hank pressed his face into the blanket and let the tears come. Quiet tears, the kind that happen in the dark when nobody's watching. He cried for his mother and his father and his brothers and his horse and his truck and his bed and his life. He cried for the pot roast Hazel had made that he'd never eaten. He cried for the new bull calf he'd never see grow up. He cried for everything that was 154 years away and might as well have been on the moon.

Joshua heard him. The old man didn't say anything. Didn't offer comfort or advice or platitudes. He just let Hank cry, because Joshua had been alive long enough to know that some grief needed to be felt, not fixed.

When the tears stopped, Joshua's voice came from the cot, quiet and rough.

"It gets easier, son," Joshua said. "Not better. Just easier. Missin' people don't go away. But it turns from a knife into an ache, and an ache you can live with."

"How do you know?" Hank asked.

"Because I've been missin' people my whole life," Joshua said. "My mama. My daddy. Pete Sweeney. Friends I lost to cholera and horse falls and just plain bad luck. Every one of 'em still lives in my chest somewhere. But I'm still here. Still breathin'. Still puttin' one boot in front of the other. That's all you gotta do, Hank. Just keep puttin' one boot in front of the other."

"One boot in front of the other," Hank said.

"That's it," Joshua said. "That's the whole secret to survivin' anything. One boot. Then the next one. Then the next one. Eventually you've walked somewhere worth bein'."

Hank lay in the dark and thought about boots. His cowboy boots at home by the bedroom door. The boots Joshua had given him today, worn by a younger man's feet decades ago. Chester's boots, muddy and permanent, standing by the back door every night. Three pairs of boots across 154 years, all walking the same land, all carrying men who were just trying to get to the next morning.

"Goodnight, Joshua," Hank said.

"Goodnight, son," Joshua said.

The creek ran outside. The wind moved through the cottonwoods. The stars filled the gaps in the roof planks — more stars than Hank had ever seen, because there were no city lights for hundreds of miles and the sky was so clear and so deep that it looked like someone had spilled diamonds across black velvet.

Tomorrow he'd ride Dolly to Thamon's ranch. Tomorrow he'd meet the man who was building one of the first cattle operations in the territory. Tomorrow he'd start a life in 1870 that he never planned and couldn't explain.

But tonight, he put on Joshua's boots and they fit. And in a world where nothing else made sense, that was enough to build on.

One boot in front of the other.

CHAPTER 5: The Rancher

Dolly had two speeds — slow and slower — and she used both of them on the ride to Thamon's ranch Monday morning.

Joshua had warned him. "She ain't in a hurry and she ain't ever been in a hurry," Joshua said as he helped Hank saddle the old buckskin in the gray light of dawn. "You kick her and she'll stop altogether just to make a point. You ask her nice and she might pick it up to a trot, but only if she's decided she likes you."

"How do I get her to like me?" Hank asked.

"Apples," Joshua said. "She'll sell her soul for an apple. I ain't got any, so you'll have to rely on charm."

Hank relied on charm. Dolly was unimpressed. They covered the six miles in just over an hour, following the creek east through open grassland that rolled in every direction like a green ocean. Joshua followed behind on foot — his back wouldn't allow a horse anymore, but he could walk six miles on a good morning, and this was a good morning. Cool air, blue sky, the Bighorns white and sharp to the west.

They saw the ranch before they reached it. Not a ranch the way Hank knew ranches — no barns with metal roofs, no corrals with welded pipe, no truck parked by the gate. What Hank saw was a low log building with smoke coming from the chimney, a bunkhouse beside it that was barely bigger than Joshua's old shack, a set of rough-cut corrals made from split rails, and cattle. More cattle than Hank had seen since he left 2024. Spread across the flats east of the creek, grazing in loose groups, the dark shapes of Longhorns and crossbreeds moving through the grass with the unhurried confidence of animals that had never seen a fence in their lives.

"That's Thamon's place," Joshua said, catching up. He was breathing hard from the walk but trying not to show it. "Hundred fifty head, give or take. Brought most of 'em up from Colorado last year. Biggest operation between here and the Yellowstone."

A man came out of the log building as they approached. He was big — not tall, but wide, the kind of build that came from decades of physical work. Maybe fifty, maybe older — hard to tell with a face that had been weathered by sun and wind and Wyoming winters until age became irrelevant. He wore a broad-brimmed hat, a leather coat despite the warm morning, and a belt with a holstered revolver that looked like it had been there so long it was part of his anatomy.

"Joshua Bettington," the man said. His voice was deep and carried the flat vowels of someone who'd come from somewhere south — Texas maybe, or Missouri. "You haven't been over here since February. Thought maybe you'd died."

"Not yet," Joshua said. "Herman, this here's Hank Blankenship. He's a young fella from back East, lookin' for work. Knows cattle better than any boy his age I ever met."

Herman Thamon looked at Hank the way a man looks at a horse he's thinking about not buying. Slowly, critically, checking for defects. His eyes went from Hank's face to his hands to his boots to the way he sat in the saddle.

"How old are you?" Thamon asked.

"Seventeen," Hank said.

"Seventeen," Thamon repeated. The word sounded like a verdict. "I've got men twice your age who can barely keep a cow pointed in the right direction. What makes you think you can do better?"

"Because I've been working cattle since I was nine," Hank said. "My father runs a herd back home. I've helped with calving, branding, pasture management, herd health. I know how to read a cow — when she's sick, when she's about to calve, when she's about to bolt. And I know how to manage grazing so your grass doesn't die under your herd's feet."

Thamon's expression didn't change, but something shifted behind his eyes. The same look Chester got when one of the yearlings showed unexpected spirit — interest, carefully hidden behind skepticism.

"Manage grazing," Thamon said. "What does that mean?"

"You're running a hundred fifty head on open range," Hank said. "Right now, you've got plenty of grass. But if you keep your cattle on the same ground year-round, they'll eat it down to the dirt. The roots die, the soil washes away in the rain, and next spring you've got half the forage you had this year. You need to move your herd — rotate them between sections of range so each section has time to recover."

"Nobody does that," Thamon said. "Every rancher from here to Texas runs open range. You let the cattle go where they want."

"And every rancher from here to Texas has years where the grass gives out and they lose cattle to starvation," Hank said. He knew he was pushing — a seventeen-year-old telling an experienced rancher how to run his business. But the knowledge was real, and it came from Chester and from a century of ranching science that hadn't been invented yet. "Rotation works. I've seen it work."

He'd seen it work on his father's ranch in 2024. He couldn't say that. But the confidence in his voice came from the same place — years of watching Chester manage sixty-five head with methods that maximized the land without destroying it.

Thamon looked at Joshua. "Where did you find this kid?" Thamon asked.

"He found me," Joshua said. "Showed up at my place couple days ago. Don't ask me where he came from — I ain't sure I understand it myself. But I tested him all day yesterday and he knows what he's talkin' about, Herman. He ain't blowin' smoke."

Thamon was quiet for a long moment. He looked at his cattle, spread across the range, then back at Hank.

"I'll give you a week," Thamon said. "You work my range for a week, same as the other hands. Dollar a day plus meals and a bunk. At the end of the week, if you're worth keeping, you stay. If you're not, you go. Fair?"

"Fair," Hank said. A dollar a day in 1870 was good money — he'd read enough history to know that. Ranch hands in Wyoming Territory made between twenty-five and forty dollars a month, depending on the operation. A dollar a day put him at thirty a month, near the top of the range.

"One more thing," Thamon said. "I don't tolerate fighting, stealing, or drinking on my property. You keep your nose clean, you do your work, and you get along with the other hands. We're a small crew and we depend on each other out here. There's no law within fifty miles. We handle our own problems. Understood?"

"Understood," Hank said.

"Good," Thamon said. "Put your horse in the corral and go introduce yourself to the boys. They're in the bunkhouse."

Hank dismounted and led Dolly to the corral. Joshua followed.

"You did good," Joshua said quietly. "Thamon don't give a week to just anybody. Most men who show up lookin' for work, he gives 'em a day. You got a week. That means he's interested."

"Thanks for bringing me," Hank said.

"I'll be headin' back," Joshua said. "Six miles is about all my back's good for in one day. But Hank —" He put his hand on Hank's shoulder. The grip was strong despite the old man's age, the grip of a man who'd spent forty years holding ropes and reins. "You're gonna be fine. Just do what you know and keep your mouth shut about the rest."

"I will," Hank said.

"And come visit when you can," Joshua said. "I got used to havin' somebody to talk to besides Dolly. Gonna be quiet without you."

"I'll come every Sunday," Hank said. "If Thamon gives

days off."

"He gives Sundays," Joshua said. "Most ranchers do. Even God rested on Sunday, and He had a bigger herd than Thamon."

Joshua turned and started walking west, back toward his shack on the creek. Hank watched him go — the stiff, rolling gait, the old hat, the figure getting smaller against the enormous landscape. The first person in 1870 who'd been kind to him. The man who'd fed him and clothed him and given him boots and a chance. Walking away at the speed of bad knees and a good heart.

Hank turned to the bunkhouse. It was a long, low building with a sod roof and a plank door that stood open. Inside, the air smelled like coffee and sweat and unwashed wool. Four cots lined one wall, each with a blanket and a saddlebag. A table in the center with tin mugs and a coffee pot. A potbelly stove, cold now because it was May and the mornings were mild.

Two men were inside. One was sitting on a cot cleaning a rifle — young, maybe nineteen or twenty, lean and brown-haired, with a face that looked like it smiled easily. He looked up when Hank walked in and grinned.

"New hand?" the young man said. He set the rifle aside and stood, extending his hand. "Jim Cotton. I been here since March. Welcome to the finest bunkhouse in

Wyoming Territory, which ain't sayin' much since it's the only bunkhouse I've ever been in."

"Hank Blankenship," Hank said. He shook Jim's hand — a firm grip, callused, the hand of a working man despite his age. "Thamon gave me a week to prove myself."

"A week's more than most get," Jim said. "Last fella who showed up, Thamon took one look at him and said 'you ain't worth the beans I'd have to feed you' and sent him on his way." Jim laughed. "Herman Thamon is the fairest boss I ever had, but he don't suffer fools."

"I'll try not to be a fool," Hank said.

"That's the spirit," Jim said. He nodded toward the other man in the bunkhouse — the one who hadn't stood up, hadn't spoken, hadn't done anything except stare at Hank from a cot against the far wall.

Claven Clower.

The man was everything Joshua hadn't warned him about because Joshua had never met him. Thirty-five years old, but the kind of thirty-five that looked like fifty — rough whiskers that were closer to a beard than stubble, hair that hung past his collar in greasy tangles, clothes that had been worn so long they'd taken on the color and texture of the man wearing them. He was lean in the way that hungry dogs are lean, all angles and sinew, with hands that were permanently darkened by dirt and sun and things he'd never bothered to wash off.

And the smell. Hank caught it from across the bunkhouse — a wall of body odor and old sweat and tobacco and something sour underneath that suggested Claven Clower's relationship with water was hostile and longstanding.

"Claven," Jim said, with the careful tone of a man making an introduction he'd rather skip. "This is Hank. New hand."

Claven looked at Hank the way a coyote looks at a rabbit — not with hunger exactly, but with the automatic assessment of a predator deciding whether something was worth the effort.

"How old are you?" Claven asked. His voice was flat, nasal, the kind of voice that had never said anything friendly and probably never would.

"Seventeen," Hank said.

"Seventeen," Claven said. He spat on the bunkhouse floor — a gesture that Hank understood was commentary, not hygiene. "Thamon's hirin' children now. Must be runnin' low on real men."

"Claven," Jim said. "Come on."

"I been here three years," Claven said. He didn't

stand. Didn't offer his hand. Didn't do anything except stare at Hank with eyes that had the flat, dull sheen of a man who resented everything and everyone on principle. "Three years I've worked this range. Three years I've kept Thamon's cattle alive through winter and wolves and everything else this territory throws at you. And now he's bringin' in a boy. A boy who ain't got hair on his chin yet."

"I'm not here to replace anybody," Hank said. He kept his voice even. Chester had taught him that — never rise to a man who's trying to bait you. Let him burn his own energy while you save yours. "I'm here to work. Same as you."

"You ain't the same as me," Claven said. "You're a kid playin' cowboy. I'll give you three days before you're cryin' for your mama and runnin' back to wherever you come from."

Jim stepped between them — not physically, but with his presence, the way a man positions himself to redirect a conversation before it becomes a confrontation.

"Hank, let me show you around," Jim said. "Corral's out back, tack room's on the side, privy's fifty yards east — you'll smell it before you see it. Come on."

Hank followed Jim out of the bunkhouse, leaving Claven on his cot with his flat eyes and his smell and his three years of resentment.

"Don't mind Claven," Jim said once they were outside. "He's like that with everybody. He was like that with me when I showed up. He's like that with Thamon sometimes, which takes a special kind of stupid since Thamon's the one who pays him."

"What's his problem?" Hank asked.

"Life, mostly," Jim said. "He came up from Kansas three years ago. Don't know what he was runnin' from, but it was somethin'. He's a decent hand when he wants to be — knows cattle, can rope, rides well enough. But he's got a meanness in him that comes out whenever somebody new shows up. Especially somebody younger. Especially somebody Thamon pays attention to."

"And Thamon keeps him?" Hank asked.

"Out here, you take what you can get," Jim said. "Ranch hands don't exactly grow on trees in Wyoming Territory. Claven does the work. He does it angry and he does it ugly, but he does it. That's enough for Thamon. Barely."

They walked the ranch. Jim showed Hank the corrals, the tack room, the water troughs, the stretch of range where Thamon's herd was currently grazing. The cattle were mostly Longhorns — rangy, tough, adapted to open range — with some crossbreeds that Thamon had brought up from Colorado. They grazed in loose groups across a valley that stretched for miles, the grass thick and green with spring growth.

"How many hands total?" Hank asked.

"Four, now that you're here," Jim said. "Me, Claven, a fella named Dub Harkin who's out riding the north range today, and you. Plus Thamon himself, who works harder than any of us."

"Four hands for a hundred fifty head," Hank said. On Chester's ranch in 2024, one man could manage sixty-five head with modern equipment — trucks, ATVs, squeeze chutes, veterinary supplies. In 1870, with nothing but horses and ropes, a hundred fifty head needed more hands than four.

"It's tight," Jim said, reading Hank's expression. "That's why Thamon's hirin'. He needs at least two more. We're stretched thin, especially during roundup."

"When's roundup?" Hank asked.

"Fall," Jim said. "September, October. We gather everything that's spread across the range, sort 'em, brand the new calves, cut the steers for sale. It's the biggest job of the year and it takes weeks." He grinned. "You'll love it. Or you'll hate it. There's no in-between with roundup."

"I'll love it," Hank said. Because he did love it — he'd loved roundup on Chester's ranch since he was old enough to ride alongside his father. The work was hard and long and dirty, but there was something about gathering a scattered herd and bringing them together that satisfied a part of Hank that nothing else reached. The connection between man and animal and land. The oldest work in the world.

They spent the rest of the afternoon riding the range together. Jim showed Hank the boundaries of Thamon's operation — marked not by fences but by creek lines, ridges, and landmarks that the hands memorized. The range was vast. In 2024, Chester's sixty-five head grazed on two hundred and forty acres. Thamon's hundred fifty head roamed across thousands of acres of open range that technically belonged to nobody and therefore belonged to everyone who could hold it.

"Nobody owns the grass," Jim said. "Not officially. It's government land, open for grazin'. Thamon runs his cattle here because he was first and because he's got the muscle to keep others from pushin' in. But that won't last forever. More folks are comin' every year."

"It never lasts," Hank said. He was thinking about the history he knew — the range wars, the homesteaders, the fences that would eventually carve this open country into pieces. But he said it like a general observation, not a prediction.

"You talk like an old man sometimes," Jim said. He

was grinning, no malice in it. "Like you've seen things you shouldn't know about yet."

"My dad says I was born old," Hank said. It was the truest thing he'd said all day that didn't involve cattle management.

By the time they rode back to the ranch house at sunset, Hank felt something he hadn't felt since he landed in the meadow on Saturday. Purpose. He had a job. He had a place to sleep. He had a friend in Jim Cotton, who laughed easily and talked freely and didn't ask questions that Hank couldn't answer. He had an enemy in Claven Clower, who was going to make his life difficult for reasons that had nothing to do with Hank and everything to do with Claven's own bitterness.

And he had the knowledge — 154 years of ranching evolution stored in his head, methods and techniques that these men wouldn't discover for decades. Knowledge that could make Herman Thamon's operation the most successful ranch in the territory, if Hank was smart about how he shared it.

Not all at once. Not in ways that drew too much attention. Piece by piece, suggestion by suggestion, the way Chester had taught him — not by lecturing, but by doing. Show a man a better way and he'll adopt it. Tell a man he's doing it wrong and he'll dig in.

That night in the bunkhouse, Hank lay on his cot —
the fourth one, against the wall near the door — and listened
to the sounds of his new life. Jim's easy breathing across the
room. Dub Harkin's snoring from the cot by the stove —
Hank had met Dub at dinner, a quiet man in his forties who
nodded once and went back to his beans, which was
apparently the full extent of Dub Harkin's social interaction.
And Claven, on the far cot, silent but awake — Hank could
feel the man's eyes on him in the dark, the hostile attention
of a dog guarding a bone it didn't even want.

Through the bunkhouse wall, Hank could hear the
cattle settling for the night — the low sounds of a hundred
fifty animals finding their spots in the darkness. The same
sounds Chester's herd made at night. The same sounds cattle
had made for thousands of years. The one thing that was
exactly the same in 1870 and 2024.

He pulled Joshua's blanket tighter around his
shoulders. Touched the brim of the hat hanging on a nail
above his cot. Felt the boots standing on the floor beside
him, ready for morning.

One boot in front of the other.

Tomorrow, the work would start for real. Tomorrow,
Herman Thamon would see what Hank Blankenship could
do.

And somewhere six miles west, in a shack on Clear

Creek, an old cowboy was probably talking to his horse and missing the boy who'd fallen from the sky.

CHAPTER 6: Earning His Keep

The first week nearly killed him.

Not literally — though there were moments when Hank thought the distinction was academic. The work on Thamon's ranch was harder than anything he'd done on Chester's spread, because Chester had modern tools and Thamon had rope, horses, and the stubborn belief that anything worth doing was worth doing the hardest possible way.

There was no squeeze chute for working cattle — you roped them, wrestled them, and held on. There was no truck to haul feed — you loaded it onto a pack horse and carried it across miles of open range. There was no veterinary supply cabinet with antibiotics and dewormers — you had kerosene, salt, and whatever home remedies the hands had picked up from other ranches. And there was no ATV to check the far pastures — you rode for hours, in the saddle from dawn to dusk, covering ground that seemed to multiply every time Hank looked at it.

His body, which he'd thought was ranch-tough from years of working with Chester, discovered new definitions of soreness. His legs ached from hours in the saddle on horses that were nothing like the well-trained quarter horses he rode at home — Thamon's ranch horses were half-broke mustangs with opinions and attitudes, and riding them was less a partnership than a negotiation. His hands blistered from ropes he hadn't handled since he was twelve, when Chester had taught him to throw a loop in the corral back home. His back protested the cot in the bunkhouse, which was a marginal improvement over Joshua's floor but not by much.

But Hank worked. He worked the way Chester had built him to work — steady, thorough, without complaint. He got up before the other hands and he went to bed after them. He took the jobs nobody wanted — riding the far range in rain, checking water sources in the heat of the afternoon, mucking out the corrals while the other men sat in the shade.

And he paid attention. To the cattle, to the land, to the rhythms of an operation that was being built from nothing by a man who was figuring it out as he went.

On the third day, Hank noticed that four calves in the south section were losing weight despite good grass. He rode closer, dismounted, and checked them the way Chester had taught him — eyes, nose, gums, belly. Scours. A digestive illness that could spread through a herd like fire if you didn't catch it early.

"Mr. Thamon," Hank said that evening at the ranch house. "You've got four calves with scours in the south section. If we don't separate them, it'll go through the whole calf crop."

Thamon looked at him over his dinner plate. "How do you know?" Thamon asked.

"Checked them this afternoon," Hank said. "Watery stool, sunken eyes, dehydration starting. They need to be isolated from the healthy calves and given clean water with salt to keep them hydrated. If we can get them through the next three or four days, they'll recover."

"Salt water," Thamon said.

"It replaces what they're losing," Hank said. "It's not a cure, but it keeps them alive long enough for the illness to pass. And we need to move the healthy calves away from that ground — the sickness lives in the soil once it's contaminated."

Thamon was quiet for a moment. Then he pushed back from the table. "Show me," Thamon said.

They rode out together in the fading light — Thamon and Hank, side by side across the open range. Hank found the four calves, showed Thamon the signs, explained what he'd seen and what he recommended. Thamon listened the way he did everything — carefully, critically, missing nothing.

"Where did you learn this?" Thamon asked.

"My father," Hank said. The same answer he always gave. The truest answer he had.

"Your father must be some kind of cattleman," Thamon said. The same thing Joshua had said. The same wonder in the voice — how does a seventeen-year-old know things that men with decades of experience haven't figured out?

They separated the sick calves that night. Built a temporary pen with rope and brush — no fence posts, no wire, just what they could put together in the dark with lanterns and determination. Hank mixed salt into creek water and taught Jim how to get a calf to drink when it didn't want to — patience, a steady hand, and a willingness to get kicked.

All four calves survived. Thamon didn't say thank you — that wasn't his way. But on Friday, the last day of Hank's trial week, Thamon called him to the ranch house after dinner.

"You're staying," Thamon said. "Dollar and a half a day. The extra half is because those calves would've died without you, and dead calves cost me more than fifty cents a day."

"Thank you, sir," Hank said.

"Don't thank me," Thamon said. "Earn it."

Hank earned it. Every day, every week, through May and into June. He worked the range with Jim, riding side by side for hours, checking cattle, moving small groups to fresh grass, tracking strays that wandered too far from the herd. Jim was good company — easy to talk to, quick to laugh, full of stories about growing up in Missouri and coming west because he'd heard there was land and opportunity and he wanted both.

"My pa was a sharecropper," Jim told Hank one afternoon as they rode the north range. "Worked somebody else's land his whole life. Never owned a thing except his boots and his Bible. I swore I'd do better. Came to Wyoming because a man told me you could build something here if you were willing to work for it."

"Are you building something?" Hank asked.

"Tryin' to," Jim said. "Savin' my wages. Thamon says if I stick around long enough, he might sell me some yearlings at a fair price. Start my own herd. Small at first — maybe twenty, thirty head. Run 'em on open range alongside Thamon's, build up slow." He grinned. "Course, that's a five-year plan, and I've been here three months. Long way to go."

"You'll get there," Hank said.

"You sound awful sure about that for a kid who just showed up," Jim said.

"I know a good cattleman when I see one," Hank said. "My dad taught me that."

Jim looked at him sideways — the same look Joshua gave him sometimes, the look that said this boy knows more than he should, but I like him too much to push. "You talk about your pa a lot," Jim said. "Miss him?"

"Every day," Hank said.

Jim nodded. He didn't ask more. That was the gift of Jim Cotton — he knew where the line was and he stayed on his side of it.

The respect from the other hands came slowly but steadily. Dub Harkin, the quiet man in his forties, acknowledged Hank by starting to nod twice when he saw him instead of once. By Dub Harkin standards, this was practically an embrace. Thamon spoke to Hank directly now, asking his opinion on herd matters instead of just issuing orders.

But Claven's resentment grew in direct proportion to Hank's rising status.

The first incident was small. Hank came out to the corral one morning and found his saddle on the ground instead of on the rail where he'd left it. The cinch strap was twisted — not broken, but twisted in a way that would have loosened during a ride. If Hank hadn't noticed, the saddle would have slipped at the worst possible moment — during a gallop, or while roping, or crossing rough ground.

He straightened the cinch without saying anything. But he noticed Claven watching from the bunkhouse door with the flat satisfaction of a man who'd done something mean and was enjoying the anticipation of the result.

The second incident was worse. A gate on the south pen — the one holding the recovering calves — was left open overnight. Hank found it at dawn. The calves had wandered, but not far — he gathered them in an hour. The gate had been tied shut with a knot Hank had tied himself. Someone had untied it.

He didn't accuse Claven. He had no proof, and Chester had taught him that an accusation without evidence was just noise. But he started checking his gear twice before riding and closing gates with a double knot that was harder to undo in the dark.

The third incident crossed a line.

Hank had been riding a gray mustang named Smoke — a ranch horse that Thamon had assigned him after the first week. Smoke was young, spirited, still learning his job, but Hank had been working with him every day the way Chester worked green horses — patience, consistency, building trust one ride at a time. Smoke was coming along. He'd stopped trying to buck Hank off in the mornings and had started responding to leg pressure instead of just the reins. Hank was proud of the progress.

One morning, Smoke was agitated in the corral — stamping, tossing his head, whites of his eyes showing. Hank checked him over and found a burr shoved up under the saddle pad in a spot where it would dig into the horse's back the moment Hank's weight hit the saddle. Not a natural burr from the range — this one had been placed deliberately, pushed into the felt where it wouldn't be visible during a quick tack-up.

A burr under a saddle pad could make a horse bolt, buck, or rear without warning. On open range, miles from help, that could mean a broken neck.

Hank removed the burr. He walked to the bunkhouse where Claven was drinking coffee at the table.

"I found something under my saddle pad this morning," Hank said. His voice was even — Chester's voice, the voice of a man who was stating a fact, not starting a fight. "A burr. Placed there on purpose."

Claven sipped his coffee. "Maybe your horse rolled in it," Claven said.

"Horses don't roll burrs into saddle pads," Hank said. "And this one was pushed into the felt where I wouldn't see it during tack-up. If I'd mounted without checking, Smoke would have bucked me into the ground."

"That'd be a shame," Claven said. He didn't look up from his coffee.

Jim was in the doorway, watching. Dub was at his cot, also watching, his quiet face unreadable.

"I don't know who did it," Hank said. "But if it happens again, I'll take it to Thamon. And Thamon will handle it his way."

"You runnin' to the boss?" Claven said. Now he looked up, and his eyes had the dull heat of a man whose resentment had found a focus. "That what they teach boys back East? Run to daddy when somethin' goes wrong?"

"They teach boys back East to check their gear and solve their own problems," Hank said. "They also teach them that a man who sabotages another man's tack is a coward. Because a real man, if he's got a problem with someone, says it to his face."

The bunkhouse went very quiet. Claven's jaw tightened. His hand, the one not holding the coffee cup, moved to the table edge — not toward a weapon, but toward the leverage he'd need to stand quickly.

"I ain't got a problem with you, boy," Claven said. But his voice said otherwise. His voice said he had a problem with Hank that was older and deeper than a few weeks of working together — a problem with youth and competence and the unfairness of a seventeen-year-old being worth more than a thirty-five-year-old who'd been here three years.

"Good," Hank said. "Then we don't have a problem."

He turned and walked out. Behind him, he heard Jim exhale — the sound of a man who'd been holding his breath through a conversation that could have gone sideways.

Outside, Jim caught up. "That took guts," Jim said.

"That took patience," Hank said. "My dad always said never let a bully set the terms. You say your piece, you keep your voice down, and you walk away. If he follows, that's on him."

"And if he follows?" Jim asked.

"Then I deal with it," Hank said. "But I don't start it. Starting fights is easy. Finishing them costs more than most people want to pay."

"You sound like a preacher," Jim said.

"I sound like my dad," Hank said.

On Sunday — his first day off — Hank rode Dolly back to Joshua's shack. Six miles west, the old buckskin moving at her trademark speed of barely. But the ride gave Hank time to think, and thinking was something he hadn't had much space for during his first week of dawn-to-dark ranch work.

Joshua was outside when Hank arrived, splitting firewood with the careful economy of a man who couldn't afford to waste a swing. He looked up, saw Hank on Dolly, and his face broke into the gap-toothed grin that Hank was already learning to look forward to.

"There he is!" Joshua said. "The workin' man! Get down off that horse and tell me everything."

Hank dismounted, unsaddled Dolly, and turned her loose in Joshua's small corral. He'd walk back to the ranch this evening — Thamon's horses were available for daily work, and Dolly belonged here with Joshua.

They sat on the porch — such as it was, a single plank laid across two stumps — and Hank told Joshua about the week. The calves with scours. Thamon's trial ending with a raise. Jim Cotton's friendship. Dub Harkin's second nod. And Claven.

"The burr under the saddle pad," Joshua said. His grin was gone. "That ain't mischief, Hank. That's dangerous. A man who does that to another man's horse ain't playin' games. He's willin' to see you hurt."

"I know," Hank said.

"You tell Thamon?" Joshua asked.

"Not yet," Hank said. "I told Claven I would if it happened again."

"Don't wait for again," Joshua said. "Out here, again might mean a broken back or worse. Thamon needs to know he's got a hand who's sabotaging equipment. That ain't just about you — that's about every man on that ranch and every animal in that herd."

"I'll tell him if it happens again," Hank said. "One chance. That's what my dad would give a man."

"Your daddy sounds like a patient man," Joshua said.

"He is," Hank said. "Patience is the thing he's best at. That and raising cattle."

"And sons," Joshua said. "Don't forget sons. He raised a good one."

They spent the afternoon together. Hank chopped firewood — Joshua's back wouldn't allow it, and the pile was getting low. He patched a leak in the roof with canvas and pitch. He cleaned out the chicken coop and fixed the door on the corral gate. The same kind of Sunday work he'd do at home — maintenance, repair, the steady upkeep that kept a homestead running.

Joshua watched him work with the quiet satisfaction of a man who'd been alone too long and was remembering what it felt like to have company.

"You're good for this old place," Joshua said. "And you're good for this old man."

"You took me in when I had nothing," Hank said. "Feeding you and fixing your roof is the least I can do."

"You don't owe me nothin'," Joshua said. "What I done for you, Pete Sweeney done for me. It ain't a debt. It's a chain. Somebody helps you, you help somebody else. That's how the world works when it's workin' right."

"A chain," Hank said. He thought about Chester — the things Chester had taught him, passed down from Chester's father, passed down from his father before that. Three generations of knowledge flowing through a family like water through a creek. And now that knowledge was here, in 1870, being used on a ranch that existed a century and a half before Hank was born. The chain was longer than Joshua knew.

"I should head back," Hank said as the sun started dropping. "Six miles on foot. Need to make it before dark."

"You be careful on that walk," Joshua said. "Keep your eyes open. There's things out here besides ranchers and cattle."

"Wolves?" Hank asked.

"Wolves, bears, mountain lions," Joshua said. "And men who ain't got the manners God gave a snake. This territory draws all kinds, Hank. Most of 'em are decent. Some of 'em ain't. You stay on the creek trail and you keep movin' and you'll be fine."

Hank hugged Joshua goodbye — a brief, careful hug that the old man accepted with the awkward gratitude of a person who hadn't been embraced in a very long time.

"Same time next Sunday?" Hank asked.

"I'll be here," Joshua said. "Ain't got anywhere else to be."

Hank walked the six miles back to the ranch in the cooling May evening. The Bighorns glowed orange in the sunset. The creek ran beside him, the same water, the same stones, the same path it would follow for 154 years until it ran through a town called Buffalo where a boy named Hank had eaten breakfast with his family on a Friday morning that felt like a lifetime ago.

He thought about Chester and Hazel and Jules and Sanger. He thought about the truck he'd never drive again and the hat he'd left on a hook by the door and the bull calf from cow forty-seven that he'd never see grow up.

And he thought about Joshua. About Jim. About Thamon's ranch and the work that was hard and honest and real in a way that made everything else — the fear, the homesickness, the impossibility of his situation — manageable.

One boot in front of the other.

He made it back to the ranch before dark. The

bunkhouse was lit by a single lantern. Jim was cleaning his rifle. Dub was asleep. Claven was on his cot, staring at the ceiling.

Hank pulled off his boots, hung his hat on the nail, and lay down on his cot.

"Good Sunday?" Jim asked quietly.

"Good Sunday," Hank said.

"You walked six miles round trip to visit that old man," Jim said. "That's a lot of walkin' for a day off."

"He's worth every step," Hank said.

Jim smiled. Went back to his rifle. And Hank closed his eyes and let the tiredness of an honest day pull him under, into a sleep that was deep and dreamless and earned.

CHAPTER 7: The .44

The gun arrived on a Tuesday in June, two weeks after Hank started working for Thamon.

He didn't ask for it. Thamon brought it to him after dinner — walked up to where Hank was sitting on the corral fence watching the sunset turn the Bighorns pink, and held out a holstered revolver the way another man might hand someone a hammer.

"You need to carry this," Thamon said. "Every man on this ranch carries a sidearm. I should've given you one your first week but I wanted to see if you were staying."

Hank took it. The weight surprised him — heavier than he expected, solid in a way that demanded attention. He pulled the revolver from the holster. A Colt 1860 Army, .44 caliber, six-shot, cap-and-ball percussion. Well-used but maintained, the blue-black finish worn to silver at the edges from years of being drawn and reholstered. The grip was walnut, smooth from handling.

"You ever fired a handgun?" Thamon asked.

"No sir," Hank said. "Rifle, yes. My dad taught me to shoot his rifle when I was twelve. But never a pistol."

"Then you'll learn," Thamon said. "A rifle's for hunting. A pistol's for everything else out here — snakes, coyotes, wolves, and the two-legged kind of trouble that don't respond to polite conversation."

"Two-legged trouble?" Hank asked.

"This is open territory, Hank," Thamon said. "No law, no sheriff, no marshal. The nearest army post is Fort Fetterman, and that's a hundred miles south. Out here, a man protects himself and the people around him. You ride my range, you carry a weapon. That's not a request."

"Yes sir," Hank said.

"Jim'll show you the basics," Thamon said. "He's a fair shot. And don't practice near the herd — the noise spooks them and I don't need a stampede because a seventeen-year-old is learning to shoot."

He walked away. That was Thamon — he delivered information the way he delivered orders, in short bursts with no wasted words, and expected you to figure out the rest.

Hank sat on the fence with the gun in his hands and felt the weight of it — not just the physical weight, which was considerable, but the weight of what it meant. In 2024, guns were tools on Chester's ranch. Chester had rifles for coyotes and a shotgun for snakes and they lived in a locked cabinet and came out when needed. Hank had shot targets with his father's rifle plenty of times — tin cans on fence posts, paper targets at fifty yards. He was a decent shot with a rifle. Not great, not terrible.

But this was different. A .44 on your hip in 1870 wasn't a tool you took out and put back. It was part of you. You wore it the way you wore your hat — every day, everywhere. It meant you were a man who could defend himself and was expected to. It meant the world you lived in was dangerous enough to require it.

And it meant that someday, maybe, you might have to point it at another human being and pull the trigger.

Hank had watched hundreds of westerns. Every movie, every television show, every YouTube clip of fast draws and gunfights and showdowns at high noon. In the movies, guns were exciting. Cool. The cowboy drew fast and shot straight and the bad guy fell down and nobody had nightmares about it afterward.

Sitting on a fence in 1870 with a real Colt Army in his hands, Hank understood for the first time that the movies had lied. Not about the mechanics — about the cost. A real gun was heavy in ways that had nothing to do with ounces. It carried the weight of consequence. The weight of a decision that couldn't be undone.

He strapped the holster on anyway. Because Thamon was right — this was open territory, and a man without a gun was a man who couldn't protect the people he cared about.

Jim taught him to shoot the next morning. They rode two miles from the ranch to a dry wash where the sound wouldn't carry to the herd, and Jim set up targets — flat rocks on a dirt bank, spaced at ten, twenty, and thirty feet.

"Start close," Jim said. "Most gunfights happen within twenty feet. A man who can hit what he's aiming at from twenty feet don't need to worry about thirty."

"How do you know how close gunfights happen?" Hank asked.

"My uncle was a deputy in Missouri," Jim said. "He told me stories that would curl your hair. Said every fight he ever saw was close enough to smell the other man's breath." Jim pulled his own revolver — a Remington, newer than Hank's Colt but the same cap-and-ball design. "Here's the basics. Thumb the hammer back. That's the click — you hear it? That means it's ready to fire. Then you aim — front sight on the target, squeeze the trigger. Don't pull it, don't yank it. Squeeze. Smooth and steady, like you're milking a cow."

"Like milking a cow," Hank repeated.

"Best analogy I got," Jim said. "Now try it."

Hank drew the .44. Cocked the hammer. Aimed at the closest rock — ten feet away, roughly the size of a dinner plate. Squeezed the trigger.

The gun roared. The kick snapped his wrist back and

the barrel climbed toward the sky and the sound was enormous — not the sharp crack of Chester's rifle but a deep, percussive boom that echoed off the walls of the wash and rolled across the open prairie. A cloud of white smoke bloomed from the barrel — the black powder charge, something Hank hadn't expected. The rock was untouched. The dirt bank behind it had a hole in it approximately three feet above and two feet to the right of where Hank had been aiming.

"Well," Jim said. "You missed the rock. But you scared the hell out of it."

"The kick," Hank said. His hand was tingling, his wrist aching. "And the smoke. I wasn't expecting either of those."

"Black powder does that," Jim said. "Makes a lot of noise and a lot of smoke. You get used to it. You gotta grip it tighter. Both hands if you need to — I know the dime novels show one-handed shooting, but out here, two hands means you actually hit what you're aiming at."

He tried again. Two hands. Tighter grip. Squeezed. The .44 boomed and the smoke billowed and the rock on the left side of the target line jumped — not a direct hit, but close enough to send rock chips flying.

"Better," Jim said. "Much better. Again."

They practiced for an hour. Hank went through two full loadings — twelve shots — and reloading the cap-and-ball cylinder was a lesson in itself. Powder, ball, ram, cap — each chamber loaded individually, a slow process that Jim walked him through with patience. "This ain't a fast weapon to reload," Jim said. "Six shots is what you get in a fight. Make every one count, because you won't have time to reload."

By the end of the hour, Hank was hitting the ten-foot target consistently and the twenty-foot target about half the time. The thirty-foot target remained safe from harm.

"You'll get there," Jim said. "It's like roping. First week, you can't hit a barn. Second week, you can hit the barn but not the cow. Third week, you're roping calves like you been doing it your whole life."

"How long before I'm good?" Hank asked.

"Define good," Jim said. "Good enough to hit a coyote at twenty feet? Couple weeks. Good enough to defend yourself in a real fight? Couple months. Good enough to outdraw somebody who's been carrying a gun since before you were born?" Jim holstered his revolver. "Maybe never. But that's okay. The goal ain't to be the fastest. The goal is to be accurate enough that you don't have to be fast."

They rode back to the ranch. Hank wore the .44 on his

hip, and the weight of it against his thigh felt strange and serious and permanent — a new part of his body that he'd have to learn to live with the way he'd learned to live with everything else in 1870.

Thamon had started letting Hank take Smoke on Sundays — a small privilege that said more about Thamon's respect than any raise could. Hank rode the six miles to Joshua's shack that Sunday the way he did every week, arriving in the late morning with the .44 on his hip and a story to tell.

They were sitting on the porch of Joshua's shack, watching the evening come in across the valley, the creek running silver in the last light.

"Thamon gave you a sidearm," Joshua said. He nodded slowly. "That's right. A man on the range needs a weapon. But Hank — listen to me now, because this is important."

"I'm listening," Hank said.

"A gun ain't a toy and it ain't a friend," Joshua said. "It's a tool. Like a hammer or a rope or a branding iron. You use it when you need it and you put it away when you don't. You don't show it off. You don't wave it around. You don't threaten with it unless you intend to follow through. And if you ever — ever — point that weapon at a man, you better be ready to kill him. Because if you ain't ready, he will be, and you'll be the one in the dirt."

"Have you ever shot a man?" Hank asked.

Joshua was quiet for a long time. The creek ran. The wind moved through the cottonwoods. A hawk circled somewhere above them, riding a thermal that was invisible from the ground.

"Once," Joshua said. "Down in Colorado. Winter of '58. A man came onto the ranch where I was workin' and tried to steal horses. I was on night watch. He came around the corner of the barn and I could see he had a gun and I didn't think. I just drew and fired." Joshua's voice was even, but his eyes were somewhere else — somewhere twelve years in the past, standing in the dark outside a barn in Colorado. "Hit him in the chest. He went down. Died before sunrise."

"What did it feel like?" Hank asked.

"Like nothin' I can describe," Joshua said. "Not proud. Not sorry — he was gonna kill me if I didn't kill him. Just... heavy. Like somebody put a rock inside my chest and it never came out. I carry it around same as I carry my hat and my boots. It's part of me now."

He looked at Hank. "I pray you never have to use that gun on a man," Joshua said. "But if you do, don't be ashamed of what you feel after. Whatever it is — sick, scared, angry, numb — that's normal. That's your soul tellin' you that takin' a life costs somethin'. And a man who don't feel that cost ain't a man I want to know."

"I hear you," Hank said.

"Good," Joshua said. "Now — how's your aim?"

"Terrible," Hank said.

Joshua laughed — a real laugh, deep and warm, the laugh of a man who remembered being young and bad at things. "It'll come," Joshua said. "Shoot every day. Ten rounds. Don't waste ammunition tryin' to be fancy. Just put rounds on target, same spot, over and over. Your hand'll learn the gun before your brain does. And learn to reload fast — with that cap-and-ball, a slow reload'll get you killed."

Hank practiced every day after that. Ten rounds in the dry wash before breakfast, while the other hands were still in the bunkhouse. He'd ride out in the gray light of dawn, set up his rocks, and shoot until the chambers were empty. Day by day, the twenty-foot target went from impossible to difficult to manageable. The thirty-foot target went from fantasy to occasional. His wrist stopped aching. His grip found its shape. The weight of the .44 on his hip went from strange to familiar to part of him.

He got faster at reloading too — powder, ball, ram, cap, six times over. What took him five minutes the first day took him two minutes by the end of the second week. Not fast enough for a firefight, but fast enough that the process was automatic, his hands moving through the sequence without his brain having to direct them.

He also practiced drawing — not the fast draw of the movies, but the smooth, efficient motion of a man reaching for a tool he needed. Clear the holster, raise the weapon, cock the hammer, aim, fire. One fluid sequence. He did it a hundred times a day — dry, without loading — until the motion was in his muscles the way roping was in his muscles, automatic and reliable.

Jim watched his progress with approval. "You're gettin' better," Jim said one morning, after Hank put three consecutive shots into the twenty-foot target without a miss. "Another month and you'll be respectable."

"Respectable is good enough," Hank said.

"Respectable is what keeps you alive," Jim said. "Out here, you don't need to be Wild Bill Hickok. You just need to be good enough that the other fella thinks twice."

Claven watched too. But not with approval. Claven watched the way he watched everything Hank did — with the flat, calculating resentment of a man keeping score. Every skill Hank acquired, every compliment from Thamon, every sign of competence was another mark against the boy who'd arrived six weeks ago and was already becoming the most valuable hand on the ranch.

The sabotage continued. Small things — a water canteen emptied overnight, a rope with a frayed spot that shouldn't have been frayed, a missing stirrup leather that turned up behind the bunkhouse two days later. Nothing dangerous enough to justify going to Thamon. Just enough to remind Hank that Claven was there, watching, waiting, hating.

Jim noticed it too. "He's testing you," Jim said one evening. They were sitting outside the bunkhouse after dinner, watching the stars come out. "Seeing how much you'll take before you break."

"I don't break," Hank said.

"Everybody breaks," Jim said. "The question is how. Some men break loud — they fight, they yell, they burn bridges. Some men break quiet — they just stop caring, stop trying, give up and move on. And some men don't break at all. They just get harder. Like iron in a forge. The heat don't destroy 'em. It makes 'em stronger."

"Which kind are you?" Hank asked.

"I'm the loud kind," Jim said. "I'd have punched Claven weeks ago. That's why I admire your patience. You got a steadiness in you that ain't normal for seventeen."

"My dad's patient," Hank said. "He always said patience isn't waiting. It's knowing when to act and when to hold."

"Your daddy again," Jim said. He smiled. "I'd like to meet this man someday. He sounds like the kind of person

the world needs more of."

"He is," Hank said. And the ache in his chest — the one that never fully went away — pulsed once, like a heartbeat from across the years.

The weeks turned. June deepened into the long days of early summer. The grass grew thick on the range. Thamon's herd spread further across the valley, the calves growing strong on good forage. Hank's grazing rotation suggestion was taking hold — Thamon had divided his range into three sections and was moving the herd between them every two weeks. The grass in the rested sections was already coming back thicker than before.

"This rotation idea of yours," Thamon said one evening. He rarely praised directly, but when he acknowledged something, it meant he'd been thinking about it for a while. "It's working. The south section we rested last month has better grass than I've seen in two years."

"It'll keep improving," Hank said. "Give it a full season and you'll see the difference across the whole range."

"Where did you learn this?" Thamon asked. The same question he always asked. The question Hank always answered the same way.

"My father," Hank said.

Thamon looked at him for a long moment. "Someday," Thamon said, "I'd like to know where you really come from, Hank Blankenship. Because wherever it is, they're raising cattlemen who are fifty years ahead of the rest of us."

A hundred and fifty-four years ahead, Hank thought. But he just smiled and said, "Thank you, sir."

The .44 hung on his hip every day now. Not heavy anymore — balanced. Part of the uniform, part of the man he was becoming. He could draw and fire in under two seconds. He could hit a rock at twenty feet nine times out of ten. He could hit one at thirty feet about seven times out of ten. Not fast enough for a showdown. Not accurate enough for a sharpshooter. But good enough for a man on the range who needed to protect himself and the people around him.

He hoped he'd never have to use it on a person. Joshua's words stayed with him — the rock inside the chest that never came out. The cost that a man carries forever.

But this was 1870. And in 1870, hope wasn't a strategy.

So Hank practiced. Ten rounds every morning. Draw, aim, fire. The .44 becoming part of his hand the way the boots had become part of his feet and the hat had become part of his head.

One boot in front of the other. One round at a time.

And somewhere in the back of his mind, in the place where the movies lived alongside the reality, Hank knew that the day was coming when practice wouldn't be enough. When the rocks on the dirt bank would be replaced by something alive and dangerous and pointed back at him.

He wasn't ready for that day. Not yet.

But he was getting closer.

CHAPTER 8: Clear Creek

The first Sunday in July, Hank didn't ride to Joshua's.

He told Joshua the week before — said he needed a day to himself, just one, to think. Joshua understood without needing an explanation. "A man needs time alone with his own head now and again," Joshua said. "Don't stay in it too long, though. Your head ain't always the best company."

So instead of riding Smoke six miles west, Hank walked a mile south from the ranch to a bend in Clear Creek where a cottonwood tree had fallen across the bank, making a natural seat that overlooked the water. He'd found the spot his second week on the range and had been saving it — a place that was just his, away from the bunkhouse and the cattle and the men he worked with every day.

He sat on the cottonwood trunk with his hat off and his boots in the grass and his feet in the creek. The water was cold — snowmelt from the Bighorns, running clear over stones that had been smoothed by centuries of current. The same water that ran through Buffalo in 2024. The same creek where he'd fished with Jules last summer, where Sanger had caught a brown trout so big that Chester had made him hold it up for a photograph. The same creek that flowed past the landing zone where five of his friends had landed safely on a Saturday in May while Hank kept falling.

He'd been in 1870 for almost two months.

Two months. It didn't feel like two months. It felt like years — like the life he'd lived before the jump was a dream he'd had once, vivid and detailed but fading at the edges the way dreams do when you've been awake too long. He could still see his family's faces. Could still hear Hazel's voice calling the boys to dinner and Jules complaining about chores and Chester's boots on the porch at the end of the day. But the sounds were getting quieter. The images were getting softer. The life he'd lived for seventeen years was being slowly overwritten by the life he was living now — the bunkhouse, the range, the cattle, the .44 on his hip, the smell of black powder and horse sweat and campfire smoke.

He was forgetting. Not the people — he'd never forget the people. But the details. What did the kitchen look like at six in the morning when the light came through the east window? What did Hazel's pot roast taste like — the specific taste, not just the memory of "good"? What sound did the F-150 make when you turned the key on a cold morning? What did his bedroom look like — the posters on the wall, the spurs on the shelf, the copy of "Lonesome Dove" on the nightstand?

He was losing the details. And the details were all he had.

Hank pulled his feet from the creek and sat cross-legged on the trunk. The Bighorns rose to the west, snow still clinging to the highest peaks even in July. The valley stretched east and south, open and green, Thamon's cattle visible as dark dots scattered across the grass. A hawk circled overhead. The creek ran. The wind moved through the cottonwoods with a sound like breathing.

He thought about Chester. His father would be in the pasture right now — or in the pasture 154 years from now — checking the herd the way he did every morning. The bull calf from cow forty-seven would be two months old now, sturdy and growing, probably causing trouble the way calves do. Chester would be watching it with the quiet satisfaction of a man who loved his work and his land and his animals.

And Chester would be grieving. Because his eldest son had jumped out of a plane and never come down.

Hank thought about how Chester grieved. Not like Hazel — Hazel would cry, would talk about it, would lean on her sisters and her friends and the community that surrounded her. Chester would grieve the way he did everything else — silently, privately, the pain locked behind the same steady expression he wore every day of his life. He'd work harder. Get up earlier. Stay out later. Fill the space where Hank used to be with more labor, more fence-mending, more cattle-checking. Because Chester Blankenship dealt with pain by working through it, and the bigger the pain, the harder he worked.

Sanger would step up. Hank knew this without question. At fifteen, Sanger was already capable — strong, quiet, reliable. He'd take over Hank's chores. He'd ride the far pastures. He'd help with calving. He wouldn't complain, because Sanger never complained. He'd just do what needed doing and hope that somehow, someday, his brother would come home.

Jules would be different. Jules was twelve and loud and emotional and couldn't hide anything he felt. Jules would be angry — at Hank for disappearing, at God for letting it happen, at the world for being a place where a brother could jump out of a plane and vanish. Jules would fight about it — fight with classmates, fight with teachers, fight with anyone who said something about Hank that Jules didn't want to hear. And at night, in his room, Jules would cry. Because underneath the noise and the anger, Jules loved his big brother with the fierce, uncomplicated love of a twelve-year-old who'd never considered the possibility that his hero might not come home.

And Hazel. Mom. The woman who made breakfast every morning and ran a clothing store and managed two meddling sisters and held the family together with the same effortless authority she used to hold a kitchen together. Hazel would be the strongest and the most broken. She'd keep the house running. She'd keep the boys fed. She'd keep the store open and the bills paid and the aunts managed. But at night, when the house was quiet and the boys were in bed, she'd sit at the kitchen table and stare at the empty chair where Hank used to sit and feel the absence like a missing limb.

Hank pressed his palms against his eyes. Not crying — he was past crying. The tears had been used up in the first weeks, spent in Joshua's shack on nights when the silence was too big and the distance was too far. What was left was something drier and heavier. Not grief exactly. Acceptance. The slow, reluctant understanding that this was real and it wasn't changing and the people he loved were going to spend the rest of their lives wondering what happened to him.

He couldn't get back. He'd thought about it constantly in the first weeks — running through every possibility, every theory, every desperate idea. Jump from a high place? There were no planes in 1870, no buildings tall enough, and even if there were, jumping without a parachute wouldn't send him through time. It would send him to the ground. Find the spot where he landed? He'd gone back to the meadow twice. Stood in the exact place where his sneakers had hit the grass. Nothing happened. Just a meadow and a creek and the Bighorns and the unchanging fact of 1870.

There was no door. No portal. No button to press or

spell to speak or magic to invoke. He'd fallen through a hole in time and the hole had closed behind him.

He was here. And here was all there was.

Hank opened his eyes. The creek ran. The hawk circled. The mountains stood where they'd stood for millions of years, patient and indifferent to the problems of a seventeen-year-old boy who was 154 years from his mother's kitchen.

"Okay," Hank said. Out loud. To nobody. To the creek and the hawk and the mountains. "Okay."

Not a surrender. Something harder than surrender — a decision. The decision to stop living between two worlds. To stop splitting himself between the life he'd lost and the life he had. To stop waking up every morning hoping this was the day the dream ended and he'd be back in his bed with his boots by the door and his hat on the hook and his mother's voice calling from downstairs.

This was his life. 1870. Clear Creek. Thamon's ranch. Joshua's friendship. Jim's loyalty. Claven's hostility. The .44 on his hip and the boots on his feet and the hat on his head that wasn't the straw Resistol he'd worn every day in 2024 but was starting to feel just as much like his.

He was going to live this life. Not endure it. Not survive it. Live it. With everything he had, with every skill

Chester had taught him and every lesson Joshua had given him and every morning in the dry wash with the .44 and every day on the range with Jim and every Sunday on the creek that connected his two worlds like a thread through time.

He thought about what Joshua had said his first night in the shack. "You're here now, son. That's all that matters in the mornin'."

You're here now.

And he thought about what Joshua had said about boots. One boot in front of the other. That's the whole secret to survivin' anything. One boot. Then the next one. Eventually you've walked somewhere worth bein'.

Hank had been walking for two months. And somewhere in those two months — between the calves with scours and the Sunday rides to Joshua's shack and the mornings in the dry wash and the evenings on the bunkhouse porch with Jim — he'd walked somewhere worth being.

Not home. Home was gone. But somewhere real. Somewhere that mattered. Somewhere that was his.

He pulled a scrap of paper from his pocket — he'd torn it from the edge of a feed log in the barn, the only paper he could find. And with a pencil stub he'd borrowed from

Thamon's desk, he wrote. Not a letter — there was nobody to send it to. Just words. The words he needed to put down before they faded the way the details were fading.

Dear Mom and Dad and Jules and Sanger,

I'm okay. I know you can't hear this and I know you don't know where I am and I know that's the worst part. But I'm okay. I'm working on a ranch. I'm helping build something. I've got a friend named Jim who makes me laugh and a man named Joshua who reminds me of Dad and a boss named Thamon who's teaching me that respect is earned one day at a time.

I miss you every day. I miss Mom's cooking and Dad's silence and Jules being loud and Sanger being quiet. I miss the truck and the hat and the boots by the door. I miss cow forty-seven and the bull calf I never got to see grow up.

But I'm living. Not just surviving — living. And I think that's what you'd want me to do. I think Dad would say keep working and Mom would say keep eating and Jules would say keep being a cowboy and Sanger would just nod because Sanger knows that sometimes the best thing you can say is nothing.

I love you. All of you. And if I ever find a way back, the first thing I'm going to do is hug Mom so hard she drops whatever she's cooking and then I'm going to go to the barn and work cattle with Dad without saying a word, because that's how Dad and I talk best.

But if I don't find a way back — if this is it, if 1870 is where I stay — then I want you to know that I'm okay. I'm the rancher Dad raised me to be. Just 154 years early.

Your son and brother, Hank

He folded the paper and put it in his shirt pocket. He'd keep it there, next to his chest, the way soldiers kept letters from home. Except this was a letter to home. From a boy who couldn't send it.

The sun was past its peak, sliding toward the Bighorns. The afternoon was warm and still. Hank put his hat back on, pulled on his boots, and stood. He looked at the creek one more time — the water running over stones, heading east the way it always had, carrying snowmelt from mountains that didn't care about centuries.

"I'll be okay," Hank said. To the creek. To the mountains. To his family, 154 years away. "I'll be okay."

He walked back to the ranch. The cattle were grazing in the south section — the one Thamon had rested, the one where the grass was coming back thick and green thanks to a suggestion from a boy who'd learned it from his father in a future nobody here could imagine.

Jim was on the bunkhouse porch, cleaning his rifle.

He looked up when Hank arrived.

"Good day?" Jim asked.

"Good day," Hank said.

"You look different," Jim said. He studied Hank with the easy perception of a man who paid attention to people. "Lighter. Like you set something down."

"I did," Hank said.

"Heavy?" Jim asked.

"The heaviest thing I've ever carried," Hank said.

Jim nodded. He didn't ask what it was. That was Jim — he knew where the line was, and he stayed on his side. "Well," Jim said, "the bunkhouse is still standing, Dub's still sleeping, and Claven's still ugly. Everything's normal."

"Normal's good," Hank said.

"Normal's great," Jim said. "Now come sit down. I got a story about a mule in Missouri that'll make you laugh so hard you forget whatever it was you set down."

Hank sat on the porch. Jim told his story. Somewhere in the middle of it, Hank laughed — a real laugh, the kind that came from the stomach and shook the shoulders and sounded like a seventeen-year-old boy who was learning to be happy in a world he hadn't chosen.

The Bighorns caught the sunset and turned pink, then

orange, then the deep purple that happened nowhere else the way it happened in Wyoming.

The same mountains. The same creek. The same sky.

A different boy than the one who'd sat on a cottonwood trunk that morning, wondering if he'd ever stop missing what he'd lost.

He'd never stop missing them. That was the truth. The ache would live in his chest forever, the way Joshua's rock lived in his.

But he could carry it. The way you carry boots and hats and guns and the weight of a life that was yours whether you chose it or not.

One boot in front of the other.

Hank was walking.

CHAPTER 9: A Home for Joshua

By mid-August, Hank had saved seventy-three dollars.

He kept it in a leather pouch that Joshua had given him, tucked inside his saddlebag when he was on the range and under his cot when he wasn't. Seventy-three dollars in 1870 was serious money — more than most men his age had to their name, more than Claven probably had after three years of spending his wages on tobacco and whiskey at the trading post ten miles south.

Hank hadn't spent a cent. Thamon fed his hands — beans, biscuits, beef, coffee — and the bunkhouse was free. His clothes came from Joshua. His horse was Thamon's. The only thing he'd needed money for was ammunition, and Thamon provided that too, because a well-armed hand was a useful hand and Thamon was nothing if not practical.

So the money piled up. Dollar and a half a day, six days a week, for ten weeks. Hank counted it every Sunday morning before riding to Joshua's — not because he was greedy, but because the counting was a ritual, a small proof that he was building something in this century. That he wasn't just surviving. He was accumulating. Planning. Becoming the kind of man who could make things happen instead of just waiting for things to happen to him.

And he knew exactly what he was going to do with it.

Joshua's shack was dying. The roof leaked in three places now — Hank had patched it twice, but the canvas was rotting and the planks were warping. The walls let wind through gaps that no amount of mud and moss could seal permanently. The floor had a soft spot near the stove that would become a hole before winter. And winter in Wyoming Territory was not something you survived in a shack with a rotting roof and a soft floor.

Hank had been thinking about it for weeks — how to build a proper cabin, where to put it, what it would take. He'd talked to Jim about it on their rides across the range, and Jim had grown up around log construction in Missouri. "My pa built our house from the ground up," Jim said. "Didn't buy a single board. Cut every log from the timber on our land, notched 'em, stacked 'em, chinked 'em with mud. Took him and two neighbors about six weeks. Still standing when I left."

That was the way to do it. Not sawn lumber from a mill that didn't exist within a hundred miles. Logs. Cut from the Bighorn timber, hauled by horse, notched and stacked the way men had been building cabins on the frontier since before the revolution. You didn't need a sawmill. You needed axes, a crosscut saw, horses to drag the logs, and men willing to work.

The hardware was a different matter. Nails, hinges, a door latch, window glass, a proper stove — those things had to come from somewhere. Emmett Farley's trading post, ten miles south, carried hardware that he freighted in from Cheyenne by wagon. Not cheap, but available.

And five miles east of Joshua's shack, on a stretch of creek bank that nobody had claimed, there was a flat piece of ground with good water access and natural windbreak from a stand of cottonwoods. Public domain land. Free for the taking. All you had to do was build on it.

Hank had a plan. He just needed to tell Joshua.

He rode to Joshua's on a Sunday in mid-August, the Bighorns sharp against a sky so blue it looked painted. The summer had been good — hot days, cool nights, enough rain to keep the grass green. Thamon's herd was thriving. The rotation was working. Even Claven had been quieter lately, his sabotage reduced to dark looks and muttered complaints instead of burrs under saddle pads.

Joshua was sitting on his porch — the single plank across two stumps that served as both furniture and philosophy department. He had a tin cup of coffee in one hand and was watching Dolly graze in the small corral, talking to the horse the way he always did, a steady monologue about the weather and the price of beans and the general condition of the world.

"There's the workin' man," Joshua said when Hank dismounted. "You look like you got somethin' on yer mind. Either that or you ate somethin' disagreeable."

"I've got something on my mind," Hank said. He tied Smoke to the rail, pulled the leather pouch from his saddlebag, and sat down on the porch beside Joshua. "I want to show you something."

He opened the pouch. Seventy-three dollars in mixed bills and coins — crumpled, dirty, earned one day at a time on the back of a horse in the Wyoming sun.

Joshua looked at the money. Then at Hank. Then back at the money. "That's a considerable pile," Joshua said. "What's it fur?"

"For you," Hank said.

Joshua's coffee cup stopped halfway to his mouth. "Come again?" Joshua said.

"I want to build you a cabin," Hank said. "A real cabin. Not this —" He gestured at the shack with a respect that acknowledged what it was while being honest about what it wasn't. "This was fine for a man alone. But the roof is going and the floor's soft and winter's coming. I've seen Wyoming winters in — where I come from. They'll kill a man in a shelter like this."

"I've survived three winters in this here shack," Joshua said. His voice had an edge — not angry, but proud. The pride of a man who'd built something with his own hands and didn't appreciate being told it wasn't good enough.

"You have," Hank said. "And that's a testament to how tough you are. But Joshua — you're sixty-four years old. Your back's bad. Your knees are worse. Every winter is harder than the last one, and this shack isn't getting stronger. It's getting weaker." Hank looked at the old man. "I'm not trying to insult your home. I'm trying to make sure you're alive in the spring."

Joshua was quiet for a long time. He sipped his coffee. He looked at the shack — really looked at it, the way you look at something familiar when someone forces you to see it clearly. The leaning walls. The patched roof. The door that didn't close right anymore.

"Where would you build it?" Joshua asked.

"Five miles east," Hank said. "There's a flat stretch by the creek with good water and a windbreak from the cottonwoods. Nobody's claimed it. We cut logs from the Bighorn timber — there's good pine up in the foothills, straight and tall. Haul them down by horse. Notch them, stack them, chink them with mud and moss. Two rooms — one for you, one for me. A proper fireplace. Jim says his pa built a whole house that way in Missouri. Six weeks with enough hands."

"One fur you?" Joshua said. He looked at Hank with an expression Hank hadn't seen before — not surprise, not confusion. Something softer. Something that looked like a man who'd been given something he'd stopped believing was possible.

"I need a place to come home to," Hank said. "The bunkhouse is fine for working days, but it's not home. It's just a building with cots. I want a home. And I want it to be with you."

Joshua set his coffee cup on the porch. He took off his hat — something he almost never did — and rubbed his white hair with one gnarled hand. His eyes were bright in a way that had nothing to do with the sun.

"In sixty-four years," Joshua said, "nobody's ever done nothin' like this fur me. I spent twenty years workin' other men's cattle on other men's land. I came to this creek because I had nowhere else to go and no money to go there with. I built this shack because it was all I could build alone. And I've been sittin' on this porch fur three years waitin' to die, if I'm bein' honest about it. Just waitin'. Because what else was there?"

He looked at Hank. "Then you fell out of the sky," Joshua said. "In yer bedsheet clothes and yer funny shoes.

And you were scared and lost and you didn't belong here. But I fed you and you stayed and you started workin' and you started comin' back every Sunday, and somewhere in all that, I stopped waitin' to die. Because I had a reason not to."

"Joshua —" Hank started.

"I ain't finished," Joshua said. He put his hat back on — slightly crooked, the way it always sat. "You want to build me a cabin. You want to give me a home. And you want to live in it with me. Son, I don't have the words fur what that means. I never had children. Never had a wife. Never had anybody who looked at me and saw somethin' worth investin' in." His voice went rough. "Yer the son I never had, Hank Blankenship. I don't know where you come from and I don't know how you got here and I stopped carin' about that a long time ago. Yer here. Yer mine. And if you want to build a cabin, then by God, we'll build a cabin."

Hank put his hand on Joshua's shoulder. The old man's bones were thin under the shirt — the frame of a body that had been used hard for sixty-four years and was running on stubbornness and coffee. But the spirit inside that frame was anything but thin.

"We'll start next week," Hank said. "I'll ride up into the foothills and start marking timber. Jim said he'd help on Sundays. We can have the walls up before September and the roof on before the first snow."

"I'll help too," Joshua said. "Don't look at me like that — I can still swing an axe. My back don't work fur ridin', but it works fine fur choppin'. I built this shack alone. I can help build the next one."

"Deal," Hank said.

They shook on it. Not a business handshake — something warmer. The grip of two people who'd found each other in the most unlikely circumstances imaginable and were choosing to build a life together.

The cabin went up in six weeks.

It started with the timber. Hank and Jim spent two Sundays in the Bighorn foothills, marking lodgepole pines — straight, tall, the right diameter for cabin walls. They felled them with axes and a crosscut saw that Hank bought from Emmett Farley's trading post for three dollars. The work was brutal — swinging an axe into standing timber was nothing like splitting firewood, and the first Sunday left Hank's shoulders so sore he could barely lift his arms Monday morning. But the pines came down, one by one, and they trimmed the branches and cut the logs to length — sixteen feet for the long walls, twelve for the short ones.

Hauling was the hardest part. They hitched Smoke and Dolly to a makeshift log drag — two logs chained together with the timber riding on top — and pulled them down from the foothills to the building site on the creek.

Each trip took half a day. They needed forty logs for the walls alone, plus ridge poles and rafters for the roof. It took three Sundays just to get the timber down.

Joshua worked every day. He couldn't fell trees or haul logs, but he could notch. He sat on the building site with a hatchet and a drawknife and shaped the saddle notches at each end of every log — the interlocking cuts that let the logs stack tight at the corners. He'd built his shack the same way, and his notches were clean and precise, the work of a man who'd been handling tools since before Hank's grandparents were born.

"Yer grandpa would've known how to do this," Joshua said one afternoon, shaping a notch with careful strokes. "Anybody who lived on the frontier knew log work. It's a dyin' art, I reckon. Someday they'll have machines that do it."

"Someday," Hank said. He didn't mention that "someday" had already arrived 154 years in the future, where Chester's barn had been built by a crew with power tools in three days.

The walls went up log by log. Hank and Jim lifted each one into place — heaving, rolling, sweating, the weight of green timber testing every muscle they had. Joshua directed from below, making sure each log seated properly in the notches, checking for gaps, pointing out where the chinking would need to be thickest.

"Tighter on that north corner," Joshua would call up.

"You got a gap there I could stick my arm through. This ain't a birdhouse — it's gotta keep out a Wyoming winter."

The chinking was mud mixed with grass and moss from the creek bank — the same material people had been using to seal log walls for centuries. Hank packed it between every log, pressing it deep into the gaps with his fingers, smoothing it flat. It would dry hard in the summer sun and hold through the winter if the walls were tight enough.

Emmett Farley's trading post supplied the rest. Thamon sent Hank on a supply run to Farley's post midweek — the ranch needed provisions anyway, and Thamon didn't mind adding personal purchases to a work trip. Hank came back with the ranch supplies and a pack horse carrying nails, iron hinges, a door latch, a cast iron stove — not a stove pipe, a real stove with a flat top for cooking and a firebox that would hold heat through a cold night — and two panes of window glass, wrapped in burlap and carried like newborn calves.

The glass cost more than anything else — four dollars for two small panes that had been freighted from Cheyenne by wagon over two hundred miles of rough road. But Hank wanted Joshua to have windows. Real windows that let in light without letting in wind. A small thing that made the difference between a shelter and a home.

The total cost from Farley's post was twenty-one

dollars for hardware, stove, and glass. The rest of the seventy-three went for the crosscut saw, a bag of nails, and supplies — coffee, flour, salt, bacon — to keep them fed during the building weeks. Hank had sixteen dollars left over, which he gave to Joshua.

"Fur supplies," Hank said. "Coffee, flour, whatever you need."

"I don't need charity," Joshua said.

"It ain't charity," Hank said. He'd caught himself using Joshua's speech — "ain't" instead of "isn't," words shaped by the time he was living in instead of the time he'd come from. "It's rent. I'm living in your cabin. The least I can do is keep the pantry stocked."

Joshua took the money with a grumble that was mostly performance. He'd learned over the past three months that arguing with Hank about generosity was like arguing with the creek about which way to flow — pointless and exhausting.

The roof was the last piece and the hardest. Ridge poles ran the length of the cabin, supported by the gable ends. Rafters angled down from the ridge to the wall tops.

And over the rafters, split pine shakes — thin slabs of wood that Hank and Jim split from straight-grained logs with a froe and mallet, a tool and technique that Joshua taught them with the patience of a man who'd been splitting shakes since he was ten years old.

"You hit it here," Joshua said, positioning the froe on the end of a log. "One clean strike. The grain does the work. Don't fight the wood — let it tell you where it wants to split."

They split three hundred shakes. Nailed them to the rafters in overlapping rows, each one covering the gap below it, so water would run down the roof instead of through it. It took two full Sundays to finish the roof, working from dawn to dark, Hank and Jim on top nailing while Joshua handed shakes up from below.

The cabin was finished in late September. Two rooms — Joshua's bedroom on the left, Hank's on the right, separated by a main room with the stove, a table Hank had built from leftover timber, two chairs, and a shelf for supplies.

The floor was the last piece of the puzzle, and Joshua solved it. "Ain't no sense lettin' that old shack rot," Joshua said. "The timber in them walls is seasoned three years. Dry and hard. We tear her down, split the good planks, and lay 'em fur floors. Better than standin' on dirt all winter."

Before they started pulling the shack apart, Hank pried up the floorboards where his gear was hidden and bundled it all — jumpsuit, helmet, goggles, sneakers, parachute — into a canvas sack. Joshua saw him do it and said nothing. Some things didn't need discussing. They spent the rest of the Sunday pulling the old shack apart — saving every usable plank, every board that wasn't rotted through. There was enough to floor both bedrooms and most of the main room. The planks were rough and uneven and didn't match, but they were solid and dry and kept the cold ground from seeping up through their boots.The walls were solid logs, chinked tight, twelve inches thick — enough to stop any wind Wyoming could throw at them. The roof was pine shakes over pole rafters, steep enough to shed snow. The door was thick timber on iron hinges, and it closed properly and latched securely. And the windows — two small panes of glass, one in the main room, one in Joshua's bedroom — let in light that was clean and warm and didn't come with a draft.

It wasn't big. It wasn't fancy. But it was solid and warm and built by hand from the mountains that stood above it, and when Joshua walked through the door for the first time, he stood in the middle of the main room and didn't speak for a long time.

"Joshua?" Hank said. "You okay?"

"I'm standin' in my house," Joshua said. His voice was thick. "My house. With a roof that don't leak and walls that don't bend and a door that closes like a door should close. And I got a room — my own room, with a bed and a window that's got glass in it." He turned to Hank. His eyes were wet. "I'm sixty-four years old and this is the first time in my life I've had a proper home."

"It's your home," Hank said. "For as long as you want it."

"Fur as long as I'm breathin'," Joshua said. "Which might just be a considerable while longer now that I got a reason to keep doin' it."

They moved in that Sunday. Joshua carried his few possessions from the old shack — the tin cups, the skillet, the wool blanket, his rifle, a Bible his mother had given him that he'd carried for forty years. Hank brought his saddlebag, his .44, and the folded letter in his shirt pocket that he'd written on a previous Sunday by the creek.

He stored the canvas sack with his gear under his bed in the new cabin. Hidden. Safe. The only physical proof that he'd come from somewhere else.

The trading post was the last piece. Joshua had been spending his days alone for three years — working around the shack, talking to Dolly, watching the creek. Now, with the cabin built and Hank gone to Thamon's ranch six days a week, Joshua needed something to do. Not because Hank told him to — because Joshua wanted it. The cabin had done something to him. It had given him dignity. A home. A sense that his life wasn't over, that he still had value, that the world still had a use for a sixty-four-year-old man with bad knees and good stories.

Emmett Farley needed help at the trading post. He'd mentioned it during Hank's visits to buy supplies — business was picking up as more settlers moved into the valley, and Farley couldn't run the store alone. He needed someone to stock shelves, unload wagons, help customers, keep the place clean.

"The pay ain't much," Farley had said. "Fifty cents a day. But it's steady."

Joshua took the job. Three days a week — Tuesday, Thursday, Saturday. The walk was five miles each way, which was hard on his knees but manageable in good weather. On bad weather days, Hank arranged for one of Thamon's men to give Joshua a ride on a supply run.

The transformation was remarkable. Joshua, who'd been a hermit in a shack for three years, became a fixture at the trading post. He greeted customers, told stories, gave advice to young ranchers that was decades out of date but delivered with such confidence that nobody questioned it. He carried flour sacks and stacked canned goods and swept the floor and argued with Farley about the proper price of coffee beans.

He was useful. He had purpose. He had a home to go back to at the end of the day — a home with a stove that worked and a roof that held and a room that was his and another room that belonged to the boy who'd fallen from the sky and changed everything.

Hank saw the change every Sunday when he rode to the cabin. Joshua stood straighter. Talked louder. Laughed more. The man who'd been waiting to die was living instead, and the difference was visible in every gesture, every word, every gap-toothed grin.

"You did this," Joshua told Hank one Sunday evening. They were sitting on the porch of the new cabin — a real porch this time, four feet wide, with a railing and two chairs that Hank had built from leftover timber. The creek was visible through the cottonwoods, silver in the evening light. "You gave an old man a reason to keep goin'. Don't think I don't know that."

"You gave me a place to land," Hank said. "Literally. If you hadn't been there that first day — if I'd landed in that meadow and there hadn't been a shack with smoke coming from the chimney — I don't know what would have happened to me."

"You'd have figured it out," Joshua said. "Yer a

resourceful boy. But I'm glad you didn't have to figure it out alone."

"So am I," Hank said.

They sat on the porch and watched the sun go down behind the Bighorns. The same sunset they'd watched from the old shack, but different now. Better. Because the porch was solid and the cabin was warm and the two men sitting on it had built something together — not just with logs and nails and muscle, but with the kind of trust that comes from choosing each other when neither one had anyone else.

They'd built a family. Improbable, impossible, 154 years out of place. But a family all the same.

Joshua, who'd never had a son. And Hank, who was 154 years from his father.

Finding each other on a creek in Wyoming, in a year that history would barely remember, building a home that neither of them had expected to find.

CHAPTER 10: Thieves

The first cattle disappeared in early October.

Three head — two steers and a yearling heifer — gone from the south section where the herd had been grazing on the rotation's best grass. Thamon noticed on a Tuesday when the daily count came up short. He rode the section himself, checking draws and coulees where cattle sometimes wandered, looking for tracks that would tell him whether the missing animals had strayed or been taken.

He found nothing. No carcasses from predators. No tracks leading to water or shelter. No sign that the cattle had simply wandered off. Three animals, gone from open range as if the ground had swallowed them.

"Could be wolves," Dub Harkin said at dinner. It was the longest sentence Dub had spoken in a week. "Wolves'll take a steer if they're hungry enough. Drag it into the timber where you won't find what's left."

"Wolves don't take three head in one night and leave no blood," Thamon said. His face was hard — the face of a man watching his livelihood walk away and not knowing which direction it went. "And wolves don't pick the fattest steers in the section."

Nobody said what everyone was thinking. Not yet. But

it was there — the understanding that wolves weren't the problem. Men were the problem. Men who saw unguarded cattle on open range and decided to take what wasn't theirs because there was no sheriff, no marshal, and no law within a hundred miles to stop them.

Five more head went missing the following week. This time from the north section — the far range, the stretch of open grassland that bordered unclaimed territory to the east. Jim and Hank found the tracks on a cold Thursday morning — cattle tracks heading northeast, mixed with horse tracks. Two horses, maybe three, moving the cattle at a walk. Deliberate. Patient. The work of men who'd come prepared.

"They're driving them toward the mountains," Hank said. He was crouched beside the tracks, reading them the way Chester had taught him to read sign — not just the direction, but the depth, the spacing, the age. "These are from last night. The ground's still damp in the prints. Two riders, pushing five head northeast."

"How do you know it's two riders?" Jim asked.

"The horse tracks," Hank said. "See how they overlap here? That's two animals walking side by side, not one going back and forth. And the cattle tracks are tight — bunched together, moving in a line. That's driven cattle, not strays. Strays spread out. Driven cattle stay together because someone's pushing them from behind."

Jim looked at him. "You read sign like a tracker," Jim said. "Yer daddy teach you that too?"

"Yeah," Hank said. Chester had taught him to read tracks on the ranch. And the western movies had shown him the rest — how cattle thieves operated, the methods they used, how they moved stolen cattle without getting caught. But standing over real tracks in real dirt, with eight head missing and more likely to follow, the movie knowledge was becoming survival knowledge. These weren't actors on a screen. These were real men taking real cattle, and if nobody stopped them, Thamon's operation would be gutted before winter.

They reported to Thamon. The rancher listened, his jaw tight, his eyes hard.

"Eight head in two weeks," Thamon said. "At this rate, I'll lose thirty by winter. That's a fifth of my herd." He looked at his hands — the four men who stood between his operation and ruin. "Someone is stealing my cattle. And they're doing it right under our noses."

"They're coming at night," Hank said. "Two riders, probably three, moving fast and quiet. They know which sections have cattle and which don't. That means they're watching us during the day and moving at night when we're asleep."

"Then we stop sleeping," Thamon said. "Night riders. Two-man shifts. Dusk to dawn. You see anything, you fire

two shots. That's the signal."

"And if we catch them?" Jim asked.

"You stop them," Thamon said. The words were flat, final, carrying the weight of a man who lived in a territory without law and understood exactly what "stop them" meant.

Hank and Jim took the first night shift. They rode the north section under an October sky so full of stars it looked like the Bighorns had caught fire. The air was cold — not winter cold yet, but the kind of cold that reminded you winter was coming and it wasn't going to be gentle.

They rode in silence for the first hour, watching the herd, listening for sounds that didn't belong. The cattle were dark shapes against the darker grass, settled for the night, the occasional low sound of an animal shifting or breathing the only noise besides the wind.

"I've been thinking about how they're doing it," Hank said. He kept his voice low — sound carried on the open range, and if the thieves were nearby, he didn't want them knowing riders were out. "They're hitting different sections on different nights. South first, then north. They know our rotation — they're figuring out when each section is unguarded."

"Which means they're close enough to watch," Jim said.

"Close enough to see our patterns," Hank said. "And they're moving the cattle northeast, toward the mountains. There's a box canyon about eight miles that direction — I saw it when I was riding the far boundary last month. Narrow entrance, high walls, water inside. You could hold a bunch of cattle in there and nobody would find them unless they knew where to look."

"You think they're penning them?" Jim asked.

"If I was stealing cattle, that's what I'd do," Hank said. "Move them at night, five or six at a time. Hold them somewhere hidden until you've got enough to make it worth moving on. Then you change the markings on them — take a hot iron, alter the brand so it looks different. Thamon's T-bar could be turned into half a dozen other marks with a straight iron and a steady hand. Then you drive the whole bunch south and sell them where nobody knows Thamon's brand."

Jim was quiet for a moment. "Change the brands?" Jim said. "With a hot iron? I never heard of such a thing."

"Think about it," Hank said. He had to be careful here — brand alteration with a running iron was common knowledge in the 1880s and 1890s, but in 1870, cattle branding itself was still new to Wyoming. He couldn't talk about it like established fact. He had to make it sound like he was reasoning it out. "If you steal cattle with someone else's brand on them, the brand proves they're stolen. But if you change the brand — add a line here, extend a curve there — suddenly the brand looks different. It's not Thamon's T-bar anymore. It's your mark. And who's going to question it? There's no registry. No records. Just the mark on the hide."

"That's clever," Jim said. "Crooked as a snake, but clever."

"My pa used to say a thief is just a man who's too smart for honest work," Hank said. It was something Chester had actually said, and it fit 1870 as well as it fit 2024.

"So what do we do about it?" Jim asked.

"For now, we ride," Hank said. "And we tell Thamon about the canyon. If the stolen cattle are in there, we can get them back."

"And the thieves?" Jim asked.

"That depends on whether they want to fight about it," Hank said.

They rode through the night without incident. No thieves appeared, no cattle moved. But the tracks were there — the evidence of a pattern that was building, night by night, toward a confrontation that everyone on the ranch could feel coming.

Thamon listened to Hank's thinking over breakfast.

The box canyon. The possibility of altered brands. The pattern of hitting different sections to test the night riders.

"You're saying they know our schedule," Thamon said.

"They're watching us," Hank said. "They know which sections have riders and which don't. They know our rotation. They're picking the gaps."

"Then how are they getting that information?" Thamon asked. The question sat in the room like a loaded gun.

Nobody answered. But Hank's eyes moved to Claven's cot. Claven wasn't there — he'd gone out to the corral before breakfast, which was unusual. Claven was never first to the corral. Claven was barely first to the coffee pot.

"They could have a lookout," Hank said carefully. "Someone who watches the ranch from a distance and signals when the sections are clear."

"Or someone who doesn't need to watch from a distance," Jim said. He didn't look at Claven's empty cot. He didn't need to. The implication was clear.

Thamon's face was stone. "That's a serious thing to suggest," Thamon said. "Against anyone."

"I'm not suggesting anything about anyone," Hank said. "I'm saying the thieves know too much about how we operate. Either they've got someone watching from outside, or they're getting information from someone who knows our schedule."

Thamon was quiet for a long time. He stared at his coffee the way he stared at the range — looking for patterns, reading signs, calculating odds.

"Here's what we do," Thamon said. "We change everything. New schedule, starting tonight. I decide which sections get riders and I tell each man separately. Nobody knows the full picture except me. If the thieves still hit the unguarded sections after the change, we'll know the information is coming from inside this ranch."

It was smart. Simple, clean, and impossible to game unless you knew what Thamon was doing — which only the people in this room would know.

"One more thing," Hank said. "The box canyon. Eight miles northeast. If that's where they're holding the stolen cattle, we should check it. But not yet."

"Why not yet?" Thamon asked.

"If we ride out there and the thieves see us coming, they'll move the cattle and we'll never find them," Hank said. "Let's change the schedule first. See if the stealing stops or shifts. If it shifts to match the new schedule, we know the information is coming from inside. And then we know what we're dealing with."

"And then we deal with it," Thamon said.

The new schedule started that night. Thamon told each hand separately — Hank rode the north section, Jim the south, Dub the east. Claven was assigned to the west section, closest to the ranch, where there were no cattle currently grazing. A test. If the thieves hit the sections that were unguarded under the new schedule — sections that only Thamon and his individual riders knew about — the leak wasn't internal. If the thieves somehow knew to avoid the guarded sections despite the new information, then someone who'd been told his assignment was figuring out the pattern and passing it along.

Three nights passed. No cattle went missing. The herd stayed whole.

On the fourth night, six head disappeared from the east section — the section Dub had been riding, except Dub had been called back to the ranch two hours early by Thamon for a fabricated emergency with a lame horse. The east section was unguarded from midnight to dawn, and the thieves hit it precisely during that window.

"Nobody knew Dub was coming in early except me," Thamon said the next morning. His voice was quiet in a way that was more dangerous than shouting. "I told Dub at ten o'clock last night. By midnight, the east section was empty. By dawn, six head were gone."

"Dub wouldn't —" Jim started.

"Dub's been with me two years," Thamon said. "I trust Dub. Which means someone saw him ride in and passed the word. Or someone heard me tell him."

The bunkhouse walls were thin. A man lying on his cot with his ears open could hear a conversation at the table if the voices weren't kept low.

Claven had been on his cot all night. Assigned to the empty west section, he'd returned early — said there was nothing to guard, no reason to ride empty range all night. He'd been in the bunkhouse when Thamon told Dub to come in.

Nobody said Claven's name. But the silence said it for them.

That afternoon, Hank was checking tack in the barn when Claven came in. The bigger man stood in the doorway, blocking the light, his greasy hair hanging past his collar, the sour smell preceding him like a warning.

"You been talkin' to Thamon about me," Claven said. It wasn't a question.

"I haven't said your name to anyone," Hank said. It was true — he'd been careful. Suspicion without proof was noise, and Chester had taught him better than that.

"You don't have to say my name," Claven said. "I see how you look at me. How Jim looks at me. Like I'm somethin' you stepped in." He moved closer. The smell intensified — tobacco, sweat, and the deeper sourness underneath. "You think you're smart, boy. Think you know everything about cattle and thieves and how the world works. But you don't know nothin' about men like me. Men who been scratchin' and fightin' for every dollar since before you were born."

"I know you've been here three years and you're still making a dollar a day," Hank said. He kept his voice even. Chester's voice. The voice that didn't rise to bait. "And I know that's not because Thamon doesn't pay well."

Claven's face darkened. The words had landed — the implication that Claven's low wages were a reflection of his low value. True, but painful. The kind of truth that makes enemies permanent.

"Watch yourself, boy," Claven said. "This territory's a dangerous place for smart-mouthed kids who don't know when to shut up."

"I know exactly when to shut up," Hank said. "And I know when to talk. Right now I'm talking to a man who's standing in a barn threatening a seventeen-year-old instead of riding the range like he's paid to do."

Claven stared at him. Hank held the stare. The .44 was on Hank's hip. Claven's revolver was on his. The barn was quiet except for the horses shifting in their stalls, sensing the tension the way animals always do.

"You'll get yours," Claven said. He turned and walked out.

Hank stood in the barn with his heart hammering and his hand steady and the .44 untouched on his hip. He'd faced Claven down twice now — once in the bunkhouse over the burr under the saddle pad, and once here. Both times without raising his voice. Both times without reaching for the gun.

But Claven's eyes had been different this time. Not just resentful. Cornered. The flat, desperate look of a man who was being pushed toward a wall and running out of room.

Cornered men were dangerous. Joshua had told him that. Chester had told him that. Every western he'd ever watched had shown him that.

And Hank was beginning to believe that Claven Clower — the man who smelled like he'd given up on himself years ago — was not just a bitter ranch hand with a grudge.

He was helping the men who were stealing Herman Thamon's cattle. And he was getting desperate enough to be dangerous about it.

CHAPTER 11: Jim

They found Jim on a Tuesday afternoon in late October, two miles from the north boundary, lying in the grass with a hole in his leg and more blood on the ground than Hank had ever seen outside of a movie.

The horse found them first. Jim's bay mare came walking toward the ranch house just after noon, saddled and riderless, reins dragging. A riderless horse on the open range meant one of two things — the rider had been thrown, or the rider couldn't ride. Neither was good.

Thamon saw the horse from the porch and was on his own mount before the bay reached the corral. "Hank, with me," Thamon said. "Dub, stay at the ranch. Claven — where's Claven?"

"Rode out at dawn," Dub said. "Said he was checking the west section."

Thamon's jaw tightened but he didn't comment. He and Hank rode north, following the bay's back trail — hoof prints in the soft October ground, clear and fresh, leading toward the north boundary where Jim had been assigned that morning.

They found him in a shallow draw where the grass grew tall beside a dry creek bed. He was on his back, his left leg bent at an angle that wasn't natural, his hands pressed against his lower calf where the blood was coming from. His face was white — not pale, white, the color of a man whose body was losing something it needed to keep working.

"Jim!" Hank was off Smoke before the horse stopped moving. He ran to Jim and dropped to his knees beside him. "Jim, talk to me."

"Hey, Hank," Jim said. His voice was thin, reedy, pushed through clenched teeth. "I found the cattle thieves. Or they found me. Depends on how you look at it."

"Don't talk," Hank said. "Let me see the leg."

"It's bad," Jim said. "I know it's bad. I can feel the bone."

Hank pulled Jim's hands away from the wound. The blood came faster without the pressure — dark, steady, not spurting. That was important. If it had been spurting, that would mean an artery, and an artery on the open range two miles from nowhere was a death sentence. This was muscle bleeding — heavy, dangerous, but manageable if he could stop it.

The wound was in Jim's lower left calf, below the knee. Entry wound on the outside, exit wound on the inside — the ball had gone through, which was better than being lodged. But the path had taken it through the thickest part of the calf muscle, and from the angle of Jim's leg, the ball had nicked the bone on its way through. Not a clean break — a chip, maybe, or a crack. Enough to make the leg wrong in a way that time alone couldn't fix.

"What happened?" Thamon asked. He was kneeling on Jim's other side, his face grim.

"I was riding the north boundary," Jim said. He was shaking now — not from cold, from shock. His body was trying to process a trauma it had no experience with. "Saw tracks heading northeast. Fresh. So I followed them. Found four men about a mile from here, driving a dozen head toward the mountains. Our cattle — I could see the T-bar brand on the nearest steer."

"Four men," Thamon said.

"Four," Jim said. "They saw me before I could turn around. One of them — I didn't see which — fired. I felt it hit and the next thing I knew I was on the ground and the bay was running." He closed his eyes. "I tried to get up. Couldn't put weight on the leg. So I crawled here and waited."

"How long ago?" Hank asked.

"Morning," Jim said. "Four, five hours maybe. I've been trying to stop the bleeding but my hands keep shaking."

Four or five hours. Lying in a draw in October, bleeding, alone, hoping someone would notice a riderless horse and come looking. Hank felt something shift inside him — not fear, not anger. Something heavier. The understanding that the world he was living in was a world where your best friend could be shot on a Tuesday morning and lie in the grass for five hours waiting to find out if he was going to die.

"We need to get him back to the ranch," Hank said to Thamon. "Now."

"He can't ride," Thamon said.

"Then we build a drag," Hank said. "Two poles, a blanket between them, tied to a horse. It'll be rough but it's better than leaving him here."

Thamon didn't ask where Hank had learned about travois — the makeshift stretchers that armies and frontier people had used for centuries. He just nodded and cut two cottonwood poles from the nearest stand while Hank worked on Jim's leg.

Hank stripped off his shirt and tore it into strips. He needed clean cloth for bandages, and a shirt that had been worn for a day on the range wasn't clean — but it was better than Jim's blood-soaked hands. He poured water from his canteen over the wound, washing away as much blood and dirt as he could. Jim hissed through his teeth but didn't scream. Tough kid. Tougher than most men Hank had known in any century.

"I need to wrap it tight," Hank said. "Pressure stops the bleeding. It's going to hurt."

"It already hurts," Jim said. "Go ahead."

Hank wrapped the calf — firm, even pressure, the way Chester had taught him to wrap a horse's leg when it was injured. Not a horse, he reminded himself. A person. His friend. But the principle was the same — stabilize, compress, immobilize. Stop the blood from leaving and keep the leg from moving.

He wished for things that didn't exist in 1870 — antibiotics, surgical tools, a hospital with doctors who understood gunshot wounds. He wished for the emergency room in Buffalo that was 154 years in the future, where Jim would have been in surgery within an hour and walking again within weeks. Here, in 1870, a gunshot to the leg was a roll of the dice. Infection could kill him. Blood loss could kill him. A bone fragment shifting wrong could kill him. The best Hank could do was keep the wound clean, keep Jim still, and hope that a twenty-year-old body was strong enough to heal what a .44 caliber ball had broken.

Thamon built the drag — two poles with a blanket lashed between them, the front ends tied to the saddle horn of his horse. They lifted Jim onto it as carefully as they could. Jim grabbed Hank's arm as they moved him, his grip crushing, his face twisted with pain he was trying not to show.

"Hank," Jim said. "If I don't make it —"

"Shut up," Hank said. "You're making it."

"If I don't," Jim said. "Tell my folks in Missouri. Tell them I was building something out here. Tell them I was close."

"You're going to tell them yourself," Hank said. "Because you're not dying in a draw on a Tuesday in October. That's not how Jim Cotton's story ends."

"How does it end?" Jim asked.

"With you on your own ranch," Hank said. "Thirty head, open range, the life you came out here to build. That's how it ends."

Jim almost smiled. Almost. The drag jerked as Thamon's horse started moving, and the almost-smile became a grimace, and the two-mile trip back to the ranch was the longest two miles of Hank's life.

They put Jim in the ranch house — Thamon's own bed, because Thamon said "a man who gets shot defending my cattle sleeps in a real bed, not a bunkhouse cot." Hank stayed with him.

The first night was the worst. Jim's fever started at sundown — the body's response to trauma, fighting infection that was already taking hold in the wound. Hank changed the bandages every two hours, washing the wound with clean water each time, looking for the signs he remembered from the one first-aid class he'd taken at Buffalo High School and the things Chester had taught him about treating injured animals. Redness spreading from the wound — infection. Swelling — normal, but too much meant trouble. Heat in the skin — fever fighting what was inside.

He had whiskey — Thamon kept a bottle in the ranch house for what he called "medicinal and spiritual purposes." Hank poured it over the wound, which made Jim nearly come off the bed.

"What are you doing?" Jim gasped.

"Cleaning it," Hank said. "The whiskey burns out the bad things in the wound. It's going to hurt but it'll keep the infection from getting worse."

"Where did you learn that?" Jim asked through clenched teeth.

"My father," Hank said. The answer that covered everything. Chester had used whiskey on horse wounds when proper medicine wasn't available. And every frontier movie Hank had ever watched showed cowboys pouring whiskey on gunshot wounds, which turned out to be based on real practice — alcohol killed bacteria, even if nobody in 1870 knew what bacteria was.

Hank sat with Jim through three nights. He slept in a chair beside the bed, waking every time Jim shifted or moaned or called out in the fever-dreams that came and went like weather. He changed bandages. He poured water into Jim's mouth when the fever made him too weak to hold a cup. He talked to Jim when Jim was lucid, telling him about Chester's ranch and the cattle and the Bighorns in 2024 — not the truth, but pieces of it dressed up as stories from "back East" that were close enough to real to keep Jim's mind off the hole in his leg.

"Tell me about yer daddy's ranch," Jim would say in the small hours, when the fever was high and the pain was a living thing in the room. "Tell me about the cattle."

And Hank would talk. About Chester's sixty-five head of mixed Hereford and Angus. About grazing rotation and calving season and the bull calf from cow forty-seven. About sunrise over the Bighorns and the smell of hay in the barn and the sound of his father's boots on the porch at the end of the day. Real things, true things, things that lived 154 years in the future but sounded exactly like 1870 because ranching was ranching in any century.

Jim's fever broke on the third night. He woke up clear-eyed and weak and hungry, which Hank took as the best sign possible. A man who wanted to eat was a man who wanted to live.

"How bad is it?" Jim asked. He was looking at his leg — still wrapped, still swollen, the bandages clean for the first time in three days because the bleeding had finally stopped.

"The ball went through your calf," Hank said. He kept his voice steady. Honest. Jim deserved honest. "It hit the bone — didn't break it, but damaged it. The muscle is torn up pretty bad. The infection's under control but it's going to take weeks to heal."

"Will I walk?" Jim asked.

"Yes," Hank said. "But Jim — I don't think the leg will ever be the same. The bone damage, the muscle — you'll walk, but you'll probably have a limp."

Jim was quiet for a long time. He stared at the ceiling of Thamon's ranch house — the rough timber, the gaps where daylight showed through. The ceiling of a building that belonged to the man whose cattle Jim had been defending when he was shot.

"A limp," Jim said.

"A limp," Hank said. "For the rest of your life, most likely."

"Can I ride?" Jim asked.

"Eventually," Hank said. "When it heals. You'll have to favor it, adjust your stirrup, build the strength back. But yes — you'll ride again."

"Then I can still ranch," Jim said. It wasn't a question. It was a decision — the decision of a young man who'd come to Wyoming to build a life and wasn't going to let a bullet stop him.

"You can still ranch," Hank said.

"Okay," Jim said. He nodded once — a small, firm nod that contained more courage than any speech Hank had ever heard. "Okay. A limp. I can live with a limp."

Hank put his hand on Jim's shoulder. His friend. The first friend he'd made in 1870 — the lean, brown-haired kid from Missouri who'd shaken his hand on the first day and said "welcome to the finest bunkhouse in Wyoming Territory." The kid who'd helped build Joshua's cabin on Sundays. Who'd taught Hank to shoot in a dry wash. Who'd ridden the range beside him through summer and into fall, talking about dreams and plans and the future they were both trying to build in a territory that had barely started to become something.

That kid was lying in a bed with a hole in his leg because men had shot him for trying to stop them from stealing cattle. Not movie men with blank cartridges and stunt coordinators. Real men with real guns who'd fired at a twenty-year-old boy and left him in the grass to bleed.

This was 1870. This was what it really was. Not the romance of the western movies. Not the adventure of dime novels and campfire stories. It was blood and pain and a friend with a limp he'd carry forever and the knowledge that the next bullet might not go through a leg. It might go through a chest. Or a head. And there'd be no doctor and no hospital and no ambulance. Just grass and sky and the sound of a man dying on open range because the territory had no law and no mercy for the unlucky.

Hank sat with Jim until morning. He watched the light come through the ranch house windows and thought about the .44 on his hip and the men who'd shot his friend and the confrontation that was coming. Because it was coming — Thamon would not let this stand. Fourteen head stolen, a man shot, the operation threatened. Thamon was a patient man, but patience had a limit, and Jim Cotton bleeding in his bed was that limit.

They were going after the thieves. Hank knew it. Thamon knew it. Everyone on the ranch knew it. The only questions were when and how and what would happen when they found them.

And somewhere in the back of Hank's mind, in the place where Joshua's words about the rock in the chest lived alongside the weight of the .44 and the memory of every western movie he'd ever watched, was the understanding that when they rode out to find the men who'd shot Jim Cotton, Hank might have to use that gun.

Not on a rock in a dry wash. On a man.

The thought made his hands shake. It made his stomach turn. It made every part of him that was still a seventeen-year-old boy from Buffalo, Wyoming — the boy who wore cowboy boots and watched westerns and ate his mother's cooking and helped his father with the cattle — want to crawl under the covers and wake up in his own bed in 2024.

But he wasn't in 2024. He was in 1870. And in 1870, when someone shot your friend and stole your boss's cattle and left a twenty-year-old kid to bleed in the grass, you didn't crawl under the covers.

You loaded your .44. You saddled your horse. And you rode.

CHAPTER 12: Claven

Hank saw it on a Sunday evening.

He was riding Smoke back toward the cabin after spending the afternoon with Jim at the ranch house. Jim was improving — sitting up now, eating solid food, complaining about being stuck in bed, which Hank took as a sign of recovery because a man who complained was a man with enough energy to be annoyed. The limp would come later, when Jim tried to walk and found that his left leg no longer did what his brain told it to. But for now, Jim was alive and awake and telling Hank stories about Missouri that may or may not have been true, and that was enough.

The sun was dropping behind the Bighorns, the sky turning the deep orange that meant cold was coming. Hank was on the trail that ran along the creek, two miles from the cabin, when Smoke's ears went forward. The horse had better instincts than most people — he heard things before Hank heard them, saw movement before Hank saw it, and right now his attention was locked on something off the trail to the northeast, behind a low rise that blocked the view from the creek path.

Hank reined Smoke to a stop. Listened. Voices — faint, carried on the evening air. Two men, maybe three. Too far to make out words but close enough to hear the rhythm of conversation.

He dismounted. Tied Smoke to a cottonwood branch and moved on foot toward the rise, keeping low, using the grass and the fading light for cover. The intelligence training that Chester had never given him but the western movies had — how to approach without being seen, how to use terrain, how to watch without being watched — was running in his head like instructions from a manual he'd memorized without knowing he was studying.

He reached the top of the rise and looked over.

Three men on horseback. Two of them Hank had never seen before — rough, trail-worn, the kind of men who looked like they'd been living on the move for weeks. Unshaven, dirty, armed. The kind of men who showed up in a territory without law and made their living from other people's work.

The third man was Claven Clower.

Claven sat on his horse facing the other two, talking in a voice too low for Hank to hear clearly. But the body language was unmistakable — this wasn't a chance meeting on the trail. This was planned. Claven was gesturing toward the south, then the north, then the east — the sections of Thamon's range. He was describing the layout. Drawing a map in the air with his hands.

One of the strangers handed Claven something. Small, folded. Money. Claven tucked it into his shirt without looking at it — the practiced motion of a man who'd received payments before and didn't need to count them in front of the people paying.

The meeting lasted five minutes. The two strangers turned their horses northeast — toward the mountains, toward the box canyon Hank had identified weeks ago — and rode away at a trot. Claven watched them go, then turned his horse south toward the ranch.

Hank lay flat in the grass and watched Claven ride past, fifty yards below him, close enough to see the expression on the man's face. Not guilt. Not fear. Satisfaction. The flat, mean satisfaction of a man who was getting paid for betrayal and felt he deserved every cent.

Hank waited until Claven was out of sight. Then he got up, walked back to Smoke, mounted, and rode to the cabin. He didn't go to the ranch. Not tonight. Tonight he needed to think.

Joshua was on the porch when Hank arrived. The old man read his face the way he always did — instantly, accurately, with the perception of sixty-four years of watching men.

"Somethin' happened," Joshua said.

"I saw Claven meeting with men on the trail," Hank said. He tied Smoke to the rail and sat down in the chair beside Joshua. "Two strangers on horseback. He was describing Thamon's range to them — showing them the sections, the layout. And they paid him. Cash."

Joshua's face went hard. The gap-toothed grin was gone, replaced by the expression of a man who'd lived long enough to know what treachery looked like and hated it every time.

"The men stealin' Thamon's cattle," Joshua said.

"The same ones who shot Jim," Hank said.

"You sure about what you saw?" Joshua asked. "Not just Claven talkin' to travelers?"

"Travelers don't pay ranch hands fur information about their boss's operation," Hank said. The word slipped out — "fur" instead of "for" — and he noticed it the way he'd been noticing it for weeks. He was talking like 1870 now. The language of this time was seeping into him the way the work had seeped into his muscles and the weight of the .44 had seeped into his hip.

"No they don't," Joshua said. "So what are you gonna do?"

"Tell Thamon," Hank said. "In the morning. He needs to know."

"And then?" Joshua asked.

"That's up to Thamon," Hank said. "It's his ranch. His cattle. His decision."

"But you'll be part of whatever comes next," Joshua said. It wasn't a question. "You and that .44 on yer hip."

"If it comes to that," Hank said.

"It'll come to that," Joshua said. His voice was quiet, certain. The voice of a man who'd lived through enough violence to know its rhythms. "Claven's been sellin' Thamon out. When Thamon finds out, he'll fire Claven. And when Claven gets fired, he'll go straight to them thieves and tell 'em everything — that Thamon knows about 'em, that you know about the canyon, that yer comin' after the cattle. They'll either run or they'll fight. And men who shoot a boy fur seein' somethin' they didn't want seen ain't the runnin' kind."

"I know," Hank said.

"You scared?" Joshua asked.

"Yes," Hank said.

"Good," Joshua said. "A man who ain't scared before a fight is either a fool or a liar. Scared means yer brain is workin'. Just don't let the scared make the decisions. Let yer trainin' make the decisions. Yer hands know that gun better than yer head does. Trust yer hands."

"You sound like you're sending me off to war," Hank said.

"I'm sendin' you off to whatever's comin'," Joshua said. "And I want you to come back from it." He looked at Hank with eyes that held everything the old man had never been able to say in sixty-four years of living alone — the love he'd found late, the son who'd fallen from the sky, the home they'd built together on a creek that ran through two centuries. "You come back, Hank. Whatever happens out there, you come back to this porch."

"I will," Hank said.

"Promise me," Joshua said.

"I promise," Hank said.

"Good," Joshua said. "Now go to bed. Tomorrow's gonna be a long day."

Hank rode to the ranch before dawn Monday morning. The air was November-cold now, frost on the grass, the Bighorns sharp and white against a sky that was still more night than morning. He found Thamon in the ranch house, drinking coffee, sitting at the table where Jim was still recovering in the back room.

"I need to talk to you," Hank said.

"Sit down," Thamon said.

Hank told him. The meeting on the trail. The two

strangers. Claven describing the range sections. The payment. The direction the strangers rode — northeast, toward the mountains, toward the canyon.

Thamon listened without moving. His coffee went cold in his hands. His face didn't change — didn't show anger or surprise or anything readable. Just the stone expression of a man processing information that confirmed what he'd already suspected but hadn't been willing to act on without proof.

When Hank finished, Thamon set his coffee down carefully, the way a man sets down something fragile when his hands want to break it.

"Three years," Thamon said. "I've paid that man for three years. Fed him. Given him a bunk. And he's been selling my cattle out from under me."

"I don't know how long he's been doing it," Hank said. "The cattle started disappearing in October. But Claven's been here three years. This could be older than we think."

"Or the thieves could be new and Claven saw an opportunity," Thamon said. "Doesn't matter. What matters is he's done it. He's taken money from men who stole my property and shot one of my hands." He stood. "Where's Claven now?"

"His horse is in the corral," Hank said. "He's probably

in the bunkhouse."

Thamon strapped on his gun belt. He did it the way he did everything — deliberately, without hurry, with the focused efficiency of a man who'd made a decision and was proceeding to execute it. "Stay here," Thamon said. "This is between me and Claven."

"Mr. Thamon —" Hank started.

"Stay here," Thamon said again. He walked out.

Hank stood at the ranch house window and watched. Thamon crossed the yard to the bunkhouse, opened the door, and went inside. Hank couldn't hear the conversation — the bunkhouse was fifty yards from the ranch house — but he could see through the open door. Thamon standing. Claven sitting up on his cot. The conversation was short.

Then Claven was on his feet. Gesturing. Shouting — Hank could hear the volume if not the words. Claven's voice, high and raw, the sound of a man who'd been caught and was trying to bluster his way out.

Thamon's voice, lower, harder. One sentence. Two. Hank saw Thamon point at the door — the universal gesture. Get out.

Claven grabbed his saddlebag. Shoved his things into it — the few possessions a man accumulated in three years of bunkhouse living. He pushed past Thamon in the doorway, close enough to bump shoulders, which was either carelessness or a deliberate provocation. Thamon didn't move.

Claven crossed the yard to the corral. Saddled his horse — fast, angry, the cinch jerked tight enough to make the horse sidestep. He mounted and turned toward the ranch house.

He saw Hank in the window.

For a moment, they looked at each other. Fifty yards apart. The seventeen-year-old who'd come from the sky and the thirty-five-year-old who'd sold his employer's cattle for cash. Two men on different sides of a line that had just been drawn.

Claven pointed at Hank. A single gesture — finger extended, arm straight. The pointing of a man marking someone for future attention.

Then he pulled his horse around and rode northeast. Toward the mountains. Toward the men who'd paid him. Toward the canyon where fourteen head of Thamon's cattle were being held with altered brands.

Thamon came back to the ranch house. His face was still stone, but his hands were shaking — the only sign that the confrontation had cost him anything.

"He denied it?" Hank asked.

"Said I was listening to a boy who didn't know what he was talking about," Thamon said. "Said you were trying to get him fired because you wanted his job. When I told him what you'd seen — the meeting, the payment, the strangers heading northeast — he said you were lying."

"And then?" Hank asked.

"And then I fired him," Thamon said. "Told him to take his things and get off my land and never come back. Told him if I saw him on my range again, I'd consider him a trespasser and treat him accordingly."

"He rode northeast," Hank said.

"I know," Thamon said. "Straight to his friends. Which means by noon they'll know everything — that we know about them, that we know about the canyon, that we're coming."

"Are we coming?" Hank asked.

Thamon looked at him. Then at the back room where Jim Cotton lay with a bullet wound in his leg. Then at the window where the open range stretched toward the mountains.

"They've stolen fourteen head of my cattle," Thamon said. "They shot one of my men. They've been using a man I trusted to spy on my operation. And now that man is riding toward them with everything he knows about how I run this ranch." He strapped on his gun belt tighter. "Yes, Hank. We're coming."

"When?" Hank asked.

"Tomorrow morning," Thamon said. "First light. I want them seeing the sun in their eyes when we ride up. And I want every man who can sit a horse armed and ready."

"That's you, me, and Dub," Hank said. "Three men against four, maybe more if they've got others we don't know about."

"Three men defending what's theirs against thieves who shot a boy for doing his job," Thamon said. "I like those odds."

"I don't," Hank said. "But I'll be there."

"I know you will," Thamon said. "You've been the best hand I've ever had, Hank Blankenship. Whatever happens tomorrow, I want you to know that."

"Thank you, sir," Hank said.

"Don't thank me yet," Thamon said. "Thank me when we've got my cattle back and those men are gone from this territory."

Hank spent the rest of Monday preparing. He cleaned the .44 — stripped it down, oiled every part, loaded each chamber with fresh powder and ball, seated the caps. He checked his tack, his horse, his supplies. He filled two canteens. He made sure his boots were tight and his hat was secure and his belt held the holster at exactly the right angle for a clean draw.

He was preparing for a fight the way Chester would have prepared — methodically, thoroughly, without panic. The same way he'd prepared for every jump with the skydiving club. Check your equipment. Know your plan. Trust your training. And accept that once you step out the door, the outcome is not entirely in your hands.

In the afternoon, he visited Jim in the back room. Jim was sitting up, his leg propped on a folded blanket, a tin cup of coffee in his hand. He looked better — color in his face, clarity in his eyes. But the leg was still wrapped and swollen and wrong, and when Jim saw Hank's face, he knew something was happening.

"Claven?" Jim asked.

"Gone," Hank said. "Thamon fired him this morning. I saw him meeting with the thieves on the trail last night — taking money, describing the range layout."

"That son of a —" Jim stopped himself. "So he was the leak."

"He was the leak," Hank said. "And now he's ridden straight to them. They know we're coming."

"When?" Jim asked.

"Tomorrow morning," Hank said. "First light. Thamon, me, and Dub."

"Three against four," Jim said. "Maybe more."

"That's the number," Hank said.

Jim set his coffee down. He looked at his leg — the leg that wouldn't hold him, the leg that had been destroyed by the men Hank was riding against tomorrow. Then he looked at Hank.

"I should be going with you," Jim said.

"You can barely stand," Hank said.

"I can shoot," Jim said. "Prop me against a rock and give me a rifle and I can shoot better than most men standing up. These are the men who put this hole in my leg, Hank. I've got a right to be there."

"You've got a right to heal," Hank said. "And I've got a right to know my friend is alive when I get back. So you stay in this bed and you wait for me."

"Like Joshua waits for you on Sundays?" Jim asked.

"Exactly like that," Hank said.

Jim was quiet for a moment. Then he reached under his pillow and pulled out his Remington — the revolver he'd used to teach Hank to shoot in the dry wash. He held it out.

"Take it," Jim said. "Six shots in yours, six in mine.

That's twelve before you have to reload. Better odds."

Hank took the Remington. It was heavier than his Colt — newer, better maintained, the weapon of a man who took care of his tools. He tucked it into his belt on the left side, opposite the .44.

"I'll bring it back," Hank said.

"You'd better," Jim said. "That gun cost me two months' wages."

They looked at each other. Two young men in a territory without law, one going to a fight and one unable to follow. The friendship between them — built on shared work and shared danger and the quiet loyalty of men who'd chosen each other — was visible in the silence.

"Be careful," Jim said.

"I will," Hank said.

"And Hank?" Jim said. "Don't hesitate. If it comes to shooting, don't hesitate. These men shot me without thinking twice. They won't give you a second chance."

"I won't hesitate," Hank said. He hoped it was true. He prayed it was true. But the truth was he didn't know. He didn't know what he'd do when the .44 was pointed at a living man instead of a rock in a dry wash. He didn't know if his hands would shake or his nerve would hold or if the seventeen-year-old boy from Buffalo, Wyoming, who'd watched a thousand westerns and practiced a thousand draws and told himself he was ready would actually be ready when the moment came.

He'd find out tomorrow.

That night, Hank lay in his bunkhouse cot with the .44 on one side and Jim's Remington on the other and stared at the ceiling.

Tomorrow he would ride toward men who had already proved they were willing to shoot. Men who now knew he was coming because Claven had told them. Men who would be armed and positioned and ready.

He thought about Chester. About what his father would say if he knew his seventeen-year-old son was about to ride into a gunfight in 1870. Chester would say be smart. Be steady. Don't do anything stupid. And come home.

He thought about Hazel. His mother would say don't go. His mother would say no amount of cattle is worth her son's life. And she'd be right. But Hazel wasn't here, and Hank was, and in 1870 you didn't let thieves shoot your friends and steal your boss's cattle and ride away free.

He thought about Joshua on the porch. "You come back, Hank. Whatever happens out there, you come back to this porch."

He thought about Jim in the back room with a hole in

his leg. "Don't hesitate."

He thought about the .44 in his hand. The weight of it. The cost of it. Joshua's rock in the chest that never came out.

Tomorrow, Hank Blankenship would find out what kind of man he was.

He closed his eyes.

He didn't sleep.

CHAPTER 13: The Range

They rode out at first light on a Tuesday morning in early November, three men on horseback heading northeast across open range under a sky that was the color of iron.

Thamon led. He rode the way he did everything — straight, deliberate, no wasted motion. His rifle was in the scabbard on his saddle and his revolver was on his hip and his face had the expression of a man who'd made his calculations and was proceeding to the answer. Behind him rode Dub Harkin, silent as always, his rifle across his lap, the quiet competence of a man who didn't talk about what he could do because he'd rather show you. And behind Dub, Hank — the .44 on his right hip, Jim's Remington on his left, twelve shots between two guns, and the sick knowledge that twelve shots might not be enough if the men in the canyon decided to fight.

They would fight. Hank knew it. Claven had been with them for at least twelve hours. He'd told them everything — that Thamon knew about the canyon, that Hank had seen the meeting on the trail, that the three of them were coming. The thieves had time to prepare. Time to position. Time to decide whether stolen cattle were worth killing for.

Men who'd already shot a twenty-year-old boy for seeing something he shouldn't have seen — those men had already made their decision.

The eight miles took an hour. The terrain changed as they moved northeast — the open grassland giving way to broken ground, low ridges, dry creek beds that cut through the earth like scars. The Bighorns rose ahead of them, the foothills climbing toward the snow-capped peaks. The box canyon was somewhere in those foothills — a narrow cut between two ridges, invisible from the flats, the kind of place you could ride past a hundred times and never notice unless you knew where to look.

Hank had found it on a boundary ride weeks ago. A slot in the rock, maybe thirty feet wide at the entrance, opening into a bowl half a mile deep with walls too steep to climb and a spring-fed creek running through the bottom. Natural corral. Perfect holding pen.

"There," Hank said. He pointed toward a break in the ridgeline a quarter mile ahead. "The entrance is between those two rock faces. Narrow going in, opens up inside."

Thamon reined up. He studied the terrain with the eye of a man who understood what ground meant in a fight. The ridges on both sides were high enough to provide cover for men with rifles. The entrance was narrow enough that three riders couldn't go in abreast — they'd have to go single file, which meant the first man in would take the first bullet.

"We don't ride in," Thamon said. "We approach on

foot. Leave the horses here behind this ridge."

They dismounted. Tied the horses to a scrub pine. Hank's hands were shaking — not a little, a lot. He pressed them against his thighs and willed them to stop. They didn't stop.

"Hank," Thamon said. He was watching him. "You don't have to do this. You can stay with the horses. Nobody will think less of you."

"I'm coming," Hank said.

"Then stay behind me," Thamon said. "Dub takes the right side, you take the left. We move slow, we stay low, we use the rocks for cover. When we get close enough to see inside the canyon, we stop and assess. If they're willing to talk, we talk. If they're not —" He didn't finish the sentence. He didn't need to.

They moved on foot toward the canyon entrance. Three men in a line, crouched behind the low rocks and scrub brush that dotted the slope. The ground was cold under Hank's boots — November ground, hard and dry, the grass brown and crunching with each step. The sky overhead was the flat gray of a day that couldn't decide between cloud and clear.

Two hundred yards from the entrance. Then a hundred. Hank could see the gap in the rock now — the narrow mouth of the canyon, shadowed, impossible to see into from this angle. If someone was positioned just inside the entrance, they'd see the three men approaching long before the three men could see them.

Fifty yards.

The first shot came from the right ridge.

The crack of a rifle split the morning open — not the boom of a .44 but the sharper, higher sound of a long gun, the report echoing off the rock faces and rolling across the open ground. The ball hit a rock three feet from Thamon and sent stone chips flying.

"Cover!" Thamon shouted.

Hank dove behind a boulder. His body moved before his brain caught up — the instinct of self-preservation overriding the paralysis of terror. He hit the ground behind the rock and pressed his face against cold stone and heard the second shot crack overhead, closer this time, the ball whining off the rock above him.

More shots. From the ridge, from the canyon entrance. Multiple shooters — three, maybe four, the black powder smoke blooming from their positions like dirty clouds. The air filled with the sulfur smell of gunpowder and the sound of lead hitting stone.

Thamon was behind a rock outcrop ten yards to

Hank's right. His rifle was up, barrel resting on the stone, and he fired — a controlled, aimed shot that was nothing like the panicked shooting from the ridge. The rifle cracked and somewhere on the right ridge a man cursed and scrambled backward.

Dub was to the right, further up the slope, behind a deadfall log that was barely thick enough to stop a pistol ball. But Dub was calm — the same quiet that defined him at the bunkhouse table was defining him now. He fired his rifle, worked the lever, fired again. Methodical. Unhurried. As if the men shooting at him were an inconvenience rather than a mortal threat.

Hank pressed against his boulder. The .44 was in his right hand — he'd drawn it without remembering the motion, the hours of practice in the dry wash turning muscle memory into automatic action. But his hand was shaking. The gun felt heavier than it had ever felt. Not the physical weight — the other weight. The weight of what it meant to point this weapon at a human being and pull the trigger.

A ball hit the top of his boulder and showered him with rock dust. Someone was shooting at him specifically — not random fire, but aimed fire from someone who could see him behind the rock.

Hank looked over the top of the boulder. Fast — a half-second glance, the way Jim had taught him. Take a picture with your eyes and pull back before they can aim at what they see.

He saw them. Two men on the right ridge, one with a rifle, one with a revolver. One man at the canyon entrance, behind a rock, rifle across the top. And further back, near the canyon mouth, a fourth figure — familiar even at a distance. Greasy hair, dirty clothes, the slouching posture of a man who'd never stood up straight in his life.

Claven.

Claven was there. With the thieves. Firing at the men he'd worked with for three years. Firing at the ranch that had fed him and paid him and given him a bunk. Whatever line existed between selling information and trying to kill people, Claven had crossed it.

Another ball hit the boulder. Closer. The man on the ridge with the rifle was dialing in — adjusting his aim, walking his shots toward the spot where Hank was hiding. One more adjustment and the next ball would come over the top of the rock instead of hitting it.

Hank raised the .44 over the boulder. Found the man on the ridge — thirty feet away, maybe thirty-five, crouched behind a pile of rocks with his rifle barrel visible. The man's body was partially exposed — his right shoulder and arm, enough to aim at.

Hank's hand shook. The front sight of the .44 wavered like a candle flame in wind. Twenty feet in the dry wash was easy. Thirty feet at a rock was manageable. Thirty-five feet at a man who was shooting at you while your hands trembled and your heart hammered and the air stank of black powder and the ground shook with every rifle shot — that was something no amount of practice could fully prepare you for.

He squeezed the trigger. The .44 boomed. Black powder smoke filled his vision, the white cloud obliterating the target for two seconds. When the smoke cleared, the man on the ridge was gone — not standing, not visible. Hank didn't know if he'd hit him or if the man had ducked.

He fired again. The second shot was better — steadier, more controlled, aimed at the rock pile where the man had been. He heard the ball hit stone.

Then he saw it. Through the thinning smoke, on the ridge, the man was moving — scrambling backward, clutching his right shoulder with his left hand. Hit. Maybe. Or maybe just diving for cover. The distance was too far and the smoke was too thick and Hank's eyes were watering from the gunpowder and he couldn't be sure.

He might have hit the man. He might have hit the rock beside him and the man was just retreating. He would never know for certain.

The uncertainty was a special kind of terrible.

Thamon's rifle cracked twice more from the right.
Dub fired three times in rapid succession — the fastest Hank
had heard him shoot. And then a sound from the canyon
entrance — a man's voice, hoarse and high, shouting
something Hank couldn't make out. A command. A retreat.

The shooting from the ridge stopped. The man at the
canyon entrance pulled back, disappearing into the shadows
of the narrow gap. On the ridge, Hank could see figures
moving — not toward them, away. Scrambling over the back
side of the ridge, out of sight.

Running.

The silence that followed was enormous. Not peaceful
— heavy. The silence of a place where violence had happened
and the air was still processing it. Gunpowder hung in the
cold November air like fog, the sulfur smell clinging to
everything.

"Hold position," Thamon called. "Nobody moves until
I say."

They waited. Five minutes. Ten. The ridge was empty.
The canyon entrance was dark and still. No more shots. No
more voices. Just the wind and the fading smell of powder
and the distant sound of hooves — horses, multiple, heading
northeast into the mountains. Away.

"Clear," Thamon said. He stood from behind his rock,

rifle still raised, scanning the ridges. "Dub, check the right side. Hank, with me."

Hank stood. His legs barely held him. The .44 was still in his hand, four rounds remaining. Jim's Remington was unfired on his left hip — he'd never reached for it. Six shots in the .44 had been enough. Or not enough. He didn't know. He didn't know anything except that the shooting had stopped and he was alive and the man on the ridge might have his bullet in his shoulder.

They approached the canyon entrance carefully. Thamon went first, rifle up, moving the way a man moves when he expects to be shot at — slow, low, eyes everywhere. Hank followed, the .44 in front of him, his hands still shaking but less now. The shaking was moving from his hands to his stomach, which was worse.

Inside the canyon entrance, behind the rock where the shooter had been positioned, they found a body.

The man was on his back, eyes open, a hole in his chest. Thamon's rifle shot — the one Hank had heard during the fight. A clean hit from seventy feet through a gap in the rocks. The man was maybe forty, bearded, wearing the trail-worn clothes of someone who'd been living rough for weeks. His rifle was on the ground beside him, still loaded.

Hank looked at the dead man and felt everything the western movies had never shown him. The stillness. The absolute, irreversible stillness of a human being who'd been alive five minutes ago and wasn't anymore. The eyes that were open but didn't see. The mouth that was slightly open, as if the man had been about to say something and never finished. The blood — not bright movie blood but dark, almost black, pooling on the rock beneath him.

This was death. Real death. The kind that didn't cut to the next scene or fade to black or end with credits rolling.

"Don't look at it too long," Thamon said. His voice was steady but quiet — the voice of a man who'd seen this before and never gotten used to it. "It doesn't get easier with looking."

They found the second body on the right ridge. Dub had found it first — he was standing over it when Hank and Thamon climbed up. Another man, younger than the first, sprawled behind the rock pile where he'd been shooting. Dub's rifle shot had taken him in the neck. He'd died fast — the ground beneath him told that story.

Two dead. At least two more had fled into the mountains, plus Claven. The shooting Hank had done — the man grabbing his shoulder — that man was gone. Either wounded and running or unhurt and running. Hank would never know.

"The cattle," Thamon said. He was back to business — the rancher, not the fighter. The fight was over and the work remained.

They entered the canyon. Inside, the box opened up into the bowl Hank had described — half a mile deep, steep walls, the spring-fed creek running through the bottom. And cattle. Thamon's cattle. Fourteen head, maybe more — it was hard to count from the entrance. They were grazing on the canyon grass, unbothered by the gunfire that had echoed above them, because cattle didn't care about human violence as long as the grass was good.

Hank saw the brands. Some of them were still Thamon's T-bar. Others had been altered — a straight line added to the T, turning it into a crude F. The work of a hot iron held by someone who knew what they were doing. Just as Hank had predicted weeks ago.

"Altered brands," Thamon said. He was looking at the same thing Hank was looking at. "You were right about that too."

"I wish I'd been wrong," Hank said.

They'd sort the cattle later. Drive them back to the ranch. Restore the brands or mark them fresh. The practical work of recovering what had been stolen. But right now, standing at the edge of a canyon with two dead men behind him and the smell of gunpowder still in his clothes, Hank

didn't care about cattle.

He walked away from Thamon and Dub. Walked to the far side of the ridge, where nobody could see him. Found a rock. Leaned against it.

And threw up.

Everything he'd eaten that morning — which wasn't much, because his stomach had been knotted since before dawn — came up and out and onto the ground, and after the food was gone, the dry heaves continued, his body expelling something that wasn't physical. The horror. The reality. The understanding that he'd pointed a gun at a human being and pulled the trigger and a man might be carrying his bullet in his shoulder right now, bleeding and running into the mountains.

Two men were dead. Not by his hand — Thamon and Dub had done that. But Hank had been part of the fight. He'd fired his weapon at living men. He'd contributed to the violence that had ended two lives and would scar the rest.

He pressed his forehead against the cold rock and shook. Not crying — something beyond crying. The full-body trembling of a seventeen-year-old boy who'd just lived through his first gunfight and discovered that everything the movies had taught him about the West was wrong.

In the movies, the hero shot the bad guys and the bad guys fell and the hero walked away without a scratch on his conscience. In reality, the bad guys were men. Men with faces and boots and rifles they'd loaded that morning without knowing it was the last morning. Men who'd made bad choices — stealing cattle, shooting Jim, following Claven's information — and paid for those choices with everything they had.

And Hank had pulled the trigger. Had aimed at a man's body and squeezed and felt the .44 kick in his hand and watched through the smoke to see if the man fell. He'd done that. The boy from Buffalo, Wyoming, who ate his mother's cooking and helped his father with cattle and jumped out of planes for fun — that boy had shot at a human being.

Joshua's voice in his head: "A man who don't feel sick after shooting another man ain't a man worth knowing."

Hank felt sick. He felt sick in a way that he knew would never fully go away. The rock in the chest that Joshua had described — the one from Colorado in 1858 — Hank could feel it forming inside him now. Small and heavy and permanent. A piece of this day that would live inside him for the rest of his life.

"Hank." Thamon's voice, behind him. Not harsh. Not impatient. The voice of a man who understood what was happening because he'd been through it himself.

"I'm okay," Hank said. He wasn't. But the words were

what you said.

"No, you're not," Thamon said. "And that's all right. A man who walks away from a fight feeling fine isn't a man I want on my ranch." He put his hand on Hank's shoulder — brief, firm, the same gesture Chester used. The universal language of men who didn't have the words for comfort but had the hands for it. "You did what needed doing. You stood your ground. You fired when fired upon. And your shots drove that man off the ridge — hit or not, he stopped shooting because of you."

"Two men are dead," Hank said.

"Two men who stole my cattle and shot my hand and chose to fight instead of surrender," Thamon said. "They made their choice, Hank. We made ours. The difference is we're standing here and they're not, and I'd rather be standing."

"I know," Hank said. "I just — I need a minute."

"Take all the minutes you need," Thamon said. "Then come help me drive these cattle home."

Thamon walked away. Hank stood behind the rock with his forehead against the cold stone and breathed. In and out. The November air sharp in his lungs. The smell of powder fading. The sound of cattle in the canyon below, lowing and grazing, indifferent to the blood that had been spilled on the rock above them.

He reached into his shirt pocket. The folded letter was there — the one he'd written on a Sunday by the creek, the letter to his family that could never be sent. He didn't read it. He just touched it. Felt the paper against his fingers. The connection to the people he loved, the world he'd come from, the boy he'd been before this morning.

That boy was gone. Not dead — changed. The way metal changes when you put it in a forge. The heat doesn't destroy it. It makes it something else. Something harder. Something that carries the shape of the fire forever.

He put the letter back in his pocket. He wiped his mouth. He stood up straight.

Then he walked back to the canyon, mounted Smoke, and helped Thamon and Dub drive fourteen head of cattle out of the box canyon and back toward the ranch, the November sky gray above them and the Bighorns white and silent and the open range stretching in every direction without a fence or a law or a movie screen to make it anything other than what it was.

Real. Hard. Unforgiving.

And his.

That night, in the bunkhouse, Hank lay on his cot and stared at the ceiling and waited for sleep that wouldn't come. The .44 was under his pillow — cleaned and reloaded, because Thamon had taught him that a weapon was always ready. Jim's Remington was on the shelf above the cot, unfired and returned with thanks that were bigger than words.

The nightmares came at three in the morning. Not sleep-nightmares — the kind that come when you're almost asleep and your body jerks awake. The man on the ridge, grabbing his shoulder. The smoke. The sound of the .44 in his hand. The not-knowing — did the ball hit flesh or rock? Was the man alive or dead? Would Hank carry that question for the rest of his life?

He would. He knew it already. The question would live in him the way Joshua's rock lived in him. The cost of pulling the trigger, even when pulling the trigger was the right thing to do.

He touched the .44 under his pillow. The cold metal. The walnut grip. The tool that had become part of him and would never feel the same again.

Joshua was right. A gun wasn't a toy and it wasn't a friend. It was a tool. And the man who used it carried the cost forever.

One boot in front of the other. One day at a time. One nightmare at a time.

The ceiling of the bunkhouse was dark above him. The Bighorns were invisible outside the window. And somewhere in the mountains to the northeast, a man — maybe alive, maybe dead, maybe carrying a .44 ball in his shoulder — was running through the dark with the taste of a fight he'd lost.

Hank closed his eyes. The nightmares came again.

They would come again tomorrow. And the day after that. And the day after that.

That was the cost. And Hank was paying it.

CHAPTER 14: After the Guns

Five days after the canyon, the nightmares were still coming.

Every night, different details, same core. The smoke. The man on the ridge. The shoulder. Sometimes the man fell and sometimes he didn't. Sometimes his face was a stranger's and sometimes it was Claven's. And once — in the worst dream of the five nights — the face was Chester's. Hank's father, standing on the ridge in 1870, looking at his son through the gunsmoke with an expression that wasn't anger or pain but disappointment. The disappointment of a man who'd raised his boy to work cattle, not shoot at people.

Hank woke from that one with tears on his face and his hands shaking so badly he couldn't hold the tin cup of water he poured from the bucket by the stove.

During the day, he worked. The ranch didn't stop for nightmares. Thamon's cattle needed tending, the range needed riding, the work of November — preparing for winter, moving the herd to sheltered ground, stockpiling hay — went on regardless of what happened inside Hank's head when the sun went down. He rode Smoke, he checked cattle, he mended fence. The physical work was a relief — a way to burn the energy that the nightmares created, a way to exhaust his body so completely that sleep came faster, even if the dreams were waiting when it did.

But the .44 was different now. It hung on his hip the same way it always had — balanced, familiar, part of him. But every time his hand brushed the grip, his fingers tingled. A ghost sensation. The memory of recoil. The memory of aiming at something that wasn't a rock.

He couldn't practice. That was the hardest part. He'd been shooting ten rounds every morning in the dry wash — the routine that had made him competent, the discipline that Joshua had insisted on. But the morning after the fight, when he'd ridden to the wash and drawn the .44 and aimed at the rock on the dirt bank, his hands had shaken so badly that the first shot went into the sky and the second hit the ground ten feet in front of him.

He'd holstered the gun and ridden back to the ranch without firing another round. He hadn't been back to the dry wash since.

Jim noticed. Of course Jim noticed — Jim noticed everything, even from a bed in the back room with a hole in his leg.

"You haven't been to see me in three days," Jim said when Hank finally came to the ranch house on Thursday. Jim was sitting up, his leg propped on pillows, a cup of coffee in his hand. He looked better — color in his face, clarity in his eyes, the sharp humor returning. But he watched Hank the way you watch someone who's carrying something heavy and trying not to show it.

"I'm sorry," Hank said. "I should have come sooner."

"You should have," Jim said. "Now sit down and tell me about it."

Hank sat in the chair beside the bed. He'd already told Jim about the fight the day it happened — a brief account, facts only, no feelings. Now Jim wanted the rest.

"I can't stop seeing the man on the ridge," Hank said. "The one I shot at. He grabbed his shoulder and went down behind the rocks. But I don't know if I hit him or if he was ducking. The smoke was too thick. And now I see it every night — the smoke, the shoulder, the not-knowing."

"And that's eating you up," Jim said.

"The not-knowing is worse than knowing," Hank said. "If I knew I'd hit him, I could deal with it. If I knew I'd missed, I could let it go. But the in-between — maybe I put a ball in a man's body, maybe I didn't — that's the part I can't get past."

Jim was quiet for a moment. He sipped his coffee. He looked at his own leg — the wrapped, damaged, permanently altered leg that the same group of men had given him.

"These men shot me," Jim said. "They shot me for seeing something they didn't want seen. They left me in the grass to bleed. If you hadn't found me when you did, I'd be dead. And when you and Thamon rode out to get the cattle back, those same men opened fire on you. They tried to kill you, Hank. They tried to kill Thamon and Dub. And you shot back."

"I know," Hank said.

"So here's what I need you to hear," Jim said. He leaned forward — slowly, carefully, the leg protesting. "You didn't ride out there looking for a fight. You rode out there to get stolen cattle back. They chose to shoot. You chose to shoot back. That's not murder. That's not even violence. That's survival. And the man you might have hit — the one grabbing his shoulder — that man was trying to kill you when you pulled the trigger. You don't owe him a sleepless night."

"My head knows that," Hank said. "My hands don't."

"Your hands will catch up," Jim said. "Give them time."

"How much time?" Hank asked.

"I don't know," Jim said. "I've never shot at a man. But I've been shot by one. And I'll tell you this — the nightmares I have aren't about the man who shot me. They're about the moment before he shot me. The moment when I saw him raise the gun and I knew what was coming and I couldn't do anything about it. That moment plays in my head every night. But every morning, it gets a little quieter. Not gone. Just quieter."

"Quieter," Hank said.

"That's all you can ask for," Jim said. "Not silence. Just quieter."

Sunday came. Hank rode Smoke to the cabin, staying Sunday night as always and riding to the ranch before dawn Monday. The ride felt longer than usual — not because of the distance but because the quiet of the open range, which had once felt like freedom, now felt like the space between the sounds of gunfire. His mind filled the silence with things he didn't want to hear.

Joshua was on the porch. He was wearing a new shirt — bought from Farley's trading post with his own wages, a small vanity that told Hank the old man was taking pride in himself for the first time in years. But Joshua's face, when he saw Hank dismount, lost its smile.

"Sit down, son," Joshua said.

Hank sat. He didn't need to tell Joshua what had happened — Joshua had heard about the fight from customers at the trading post. News traveled fast in a territory with few people. By Wednesday, every settler along Clear Creek knew that Thamon's men had ridden to a box canyon and come back with fourteen head of cattle and two dead men behind them.

"Yer not sleepin'," Joshua said. It wasn't a question.

"No," Hank said.

"Yer hands are shakin'," Joshua said.

Hank looked at his hands. They were. Not a lot — not the violent trembling of the first nights. But a fine tremor, visible in the fingers, the kind of shake that made holding a cup difficult and holding a gun impossible.

"Yeah," Hank said.

Joshua rocked in his chair — the new chair on the new porch of the cabin Hank had built for him. He looked at the Bighorns. He looked at the creek. He took his time, because Joshua Bettington had never rushed a conversation that mattered.

"I told you about Colorado," Joshua said. "The man I shot in '58. The rock in the chest."

"I remember," Hank said.

"What I didn't tell you is what came after," Joshua said. "The weeks after. The months after. I couldn't hold a brandin' iron without my hands goin' shaky. I couldn't hear a gunshot — not even from a hunter a mile away — without my heart tryin' to bust out of my chest. I dreamed about that man every night fur three months. His face. The sound he made when he fell. The way the moonlight looked on the blood."

He paused. The creek ran. The cottonwoods moved in the November wind.

"The first time is always the worst," Joshua said. "It don't get easier. Just gets more familiar. Like a sore tooth. First day, it's all you can think about. Hurts with every breath. A month later, it's still there, but you've learned how to chew on the other side. A year later, you forget it's sore until somethin' reminds you. But it never goes away. The tooth is always there."

"That's not exactly comforting," Hank said.

"It ain't meant to be comfortin'," Joshua said. "It's meant to be honest. Comfort's what people give you when they want you to feel better. Honesty's what people give you when they want you to survive." He looked at Hank. "I want you to survive this, son. Not just the nightmares — the whole thing. The guilt, the doubt, the not-knowin'. All of it."

"How?" Hank asked. The word came out smaller than he intended. The word of a seventeen-year-old boy asking a sixty-four-year-old man how to carry something too heavy for a lifetime.

"Same way you survive everything," Joshua said. "One

boot in front of the other. You get up tomorrow and you do yer work and you eat yer food and you lay down at night and if the dreams come, they come. And the next day you do it again. And the day after that. And somewhere in all that doin', the weight shifts. It don't get lighter. You just get stronger. Strong enough to carry it without it breakin' you."

"You make it sound simple," Hank said.

"It is simple," Joshua said. "Simple don't mean easy. Buildin' this cabin was simple — cut logs, stack 'em, put a roof on. But it dang near killed us both. Simple and easy ain't the same thing, Hank. They never have been."

"What about the gun?" Hank asked. "I can't touch it without shaking. I can't practice. I can't even draw without feeling —" He stopped. He didn't have words for what he felt when his hand touched the grip of the .44. Not fear exactly. More like recognition. The recognition of what the tool could do, now that he'd seen it.

"That'll pass," Joshua said. "Not today. Not this week. But it'll pass. Yer hands know that gun better than yer head does — that's what saved you at the canyon. Yer hands did what they were trained to do while yer head was screamin' at you to run. Trust yer hands, Hank. They'll come back to you."

"And if they don't?" Hank asked.

"Then you learn to shoot left-handed," Joshua said. And he grinned — the gap-toothed grin that could break through anything, even the heaviest conversation on the darkest afternoon.

Hank almost laughed. Not quite. But almost. And "almost" was more than he'd managed in five days.

They sat on the porch until the sun went down. Joshua talked about Colorado — not the shooting, but the years after. The ranch work, the cattle drives, the friends he'd made and lost, the slow process of building a life around the rock in his chest. He talked the way old men talk when they're trying to give a young man the benefit of decades without lecturing — through stories, through examples, through the quiet wisdom of having survived the thing the young man was currently surviving.

And Hank listened. Not just with his ears — with everything. The way he'd listened to Chester when his father explained calving. The way he'd listened to Jim when Jim taught him to shoot. The way he'd listened to the land when it told him where the cattle were and where the grass was good and where the water ran.

He listened to Joshua the way a son listens to a father. With trust. With gratitude. With the understanding that the old man on the porch had walked this road before him and was now walking it beside him, because that's what fathers do.

"I should go to bed," Hank said. It was late. The stars were out — the enormous, uncountable Wyoming stars that he'd grown to love even as everything else about 1870 was harder than he'd imagined.

"Sleep in yer room," Joshua said. "In yer bed. In yer home. And if the dreams come, I'm right through that wall. You holler, and I'll be there."

"You'll be there," Hank repeated.

"I'll be there," Joshua said. "I ain't losin' you to nightmares, son. I ain't losin' you to nothin'."

Hank went to his room. Lay down in the bed he'd built in the cabin he'd paid for on the creek that connected his two lives. The .44 was on the shelf across the room — not under his pillow tonight. He needed the distance. Not much. Just enough to sleep without the cold metal reminding him of what his hands had done.

The dreams came. Of course they came. The smoke, the man, the shoulder. But this time, when Hank woke in the dark with his heart hammering and his hands shaking, he heard something through the wall.

Joshua. Snoring. The steady, rattling, unmusical snoring of a sixty-four-year-old man who slept like a bear and sounded like a sawmill.

And for the first time in five days, Hank smiled. A small smile. The kind that happens in the dark when nobody's watching and the world is terrible but you're not alone in it.

He closed his eyes.

The dreams came again. They would come again tomorrow night and the night after that and probably for the rest of his life.

But Joshua was through the wall. And the cabin was warm. And the creek was running outside. And the boots were by the bed.

One boot in front of the other. One night at a time.

The weight wasn't lighter. But Hank was getting stronger.

And somewhere through the wall, Joshua snored. The most comforting sound in 1870.

CHAPTER 15: The Year

Winter came to Wyoming Territory the way winter always came — without permission and without mercy.

The first snow fell in late November, a dusting that melted by noon and fooled nobody who'd been through a Wyoming winter before. The second snow came in early December and stayed. By Christmas — or what Hank calculated was Christmas, since nobody on the ranch kept a calendar with any precision — the valley was buried under two feet of white and the Bighorns had disappeared behind a wall of gray cloud that wouldn't fully lift until March.

The cold was something Hank thought he understood. He'd lived in Wyoming his whole life — in 2024 Wyoming, where the houses had furnaces and the trucks had heaters and the worst a winter could do was cancel school and make the roads slick. He'd worked cattle with Chester in January, breath freezing in the air, fingers numb inside lined gloves, the F-150 idling nearby with the heater running for when the cold got too deep.

In 1870, there was no F-150. There was no furnace. There was no retreat.

The cold came through everything. Through the bunkhouse walls, through the wool blankets, through the leather coat Thamon had given him when the temperature dropped below zero and kept dropping. It came through his boots and his hat and the layers of clothing he wore until he looked like a walking pile of laundry. It came through the cabin walls on Sunday nights despite the tight chinking and the cast iron stove, and he'd wake in the morning with frost on the inside of the window glass and his breath visible in the room.

And he rode in it. Every day. Because Thamon's cattle didn't stop needing tending because the temperature was twenty below and the wind was cutting across the open range like a blade.

The cattle were the hardest part. In 2024, Chester moved his herd to sheltered winter pasture, supplemented their feed with hay bales delivered by truck, and kept water troughs thawed with electric heaters. In 1870, Thamon's cattle were on open range in the most unforgiving winter Hank had experienced in any century. They drifted with the wind, seeking shelter in draws and creek bottoms, and the hands rode out every day to find them, count them, and push them toward the areas where the grass was still accessible under the snow.

They lost cattle. It was inevitable — open range ranching in a Wyoming winter meant losses. A steer would drift too far from the herd and freeze in a draw. A cow would calve too early and the calf would die in the cold before anyone found it. An old animal would simply give up, lie down in the snow, and not get up. Thamon counted the losses with the grim mathematics of a man who'd built his operation expecting them — six head in December, four in January, three in February. Thirteen animals that had survived the summer and the thieves and the open range but couldn't survive the cold.

But Hank's knowledge helped. He showed Thamon how to identify the cattle that were weakening before they collapsed — the signs Chester had taught him. Weight loss in the hindquarters. A dull coat. Reluctance to move. Cattle that showed these signs were pushed closer to the ranch, where hay — cut and stacked during the summer at Hank's suggestion — could supplement their forage. The hay saved at least a dozen animals that would otherwise have joined the winter count.

"Nobody stacks hay out here," Thamon had said when Hank suggested it in August. "The cattle eat what the range provides."

"The range provides plenty in summer," Hank had said. "In winter, it provides snow. A hay reserve is insurance. You cut it when the grass is high and you feed it when the grass is gone."

Thamon had listened. He'd allocated two weeks in late

August for Hank and Jim to cut grass in the river bottom with scythes — backbreaking work that left them both staggering at the end of each day. They'd stacked the hay in loose piles near the ranch, covered with brush to keep the rain off. It wasn't much — maybe enough for thirty head for a month. But when January hit and the snow buried the range grass under three feet of white, those hay piles were the difference between losing thirteen cattle and losing forty.

"Your father's hay idea," Thamon said one February morning, watching the weakest cattle eat from the dwindling stacks. "Saved my operation this winter."

"It wasn't my father's idea," Hank said. Then caught himself. "I mean — it was his practice. Where I come from, everyone does it."

"Where you come from," Thamon said. The familiar phrase. The question he'd stopped asking because the answer never satisfied him. "Someday, Hank."

"Someday," Hank said.

The winter taught Hank things no movie had ever shown him. How to ride in a blizzard — head down, trusting the horse, because Smoke could see through snow better than any human and would find the way home when Hank couldn't see ten feet in front of his face. How to start a fire in wind so strong it blew out matches before the sulfur caught — you cupped your hands into a shelter, turned your back to the wind, and nursed the flame like a newborn calf. How to read the sky for weather — the way the clouds stacked before a storm, the color of the light when the temperature was about to drop, the silence that preceded a blizzard the way silence preceded a gunfight.

He learned to sleep cold and ride colder and work in conditions that would have shut down a modern ranch for days. He learned that the human body could endure more than the human mind believed possible, as long as the mind didn't surrender first. And he learned that Wyoming in winter was the most beautiful and most terrible place on earth — the Bighorns rising white against a blue sky on the rare clear days, the snow catching the light like diamonds, the silence so complete that you could hear your own heartbeat and the creak of the saddle leather and nothing else for miles in every direction.

Jim came back to work in January. Not fully — his leg wouldn't allow full days in the saddle yet. But he could ride for a few hours, and he could do corral work, and the sight of him on a horse again — the left stirrup adjusted two inches longer than the right to accommodate the damaged leg — was the best thing Hank had seen since the fight at the canyon.

The limp was permanent. Jim had accepted it the way he'd accepted everything else in his life — with a nod and a decision to keep going. He walked with a hitch in his step, the left leg swinging slightly wider than the right, the boot landing a fraction of a second late. It changed the way he moved through the world — slower, more deliberate, every step a conscious act instead of an automatic one.

But he was Jim. The same grin. The same stories. The same easy friendship that had made Hank's first months in 1870 survivable. And when Jim sat in the saddle for the first time since October, with the bay mare steady beneath him and the open range stretching in every direction, he looked at Hank and said, "I told you I'd ride again."

"I never doubted it," Hank said.

"Liar," Jim said. And they both laughed — the real laugh of two men who'd survived the worst year of their young lives and were still standing. One of them with a limp. Both of them with scars that didn't show.

The nightmares faded. Not all at once — nothing healed all at once, Hank was learning. But gradually, the way Joshua had described it. The sore tooth that you learned to chew around. The smoke in the dreams got thinner. The man on the ridge appeared less often. The shoulder grab — the not-knowing — still came, but it came at a distance now, like watching something through a window instead of standing in the middle of it.

By February, Hank could touch the .44 without his

hands shaking. By March, he was back in the dry wash, ten rounds before breakfast, the routine restored. The shots were different now — not the eager practice of a boy learning a new skill, but the deliberate repetition of a man maintaining a tool he hoped he'd never need again. He didn't enjoy it the way he once had. But he did it. Because the territory was still lawless and the range was still open and the possibility of violence was as permanent as the Bighorns.

Joshua thrived through the winter. The new cabin held — the log walls stopped the wind, the cast iron stove kept the rooms warm, and the pine shake roof shed snow the way Hank had designed it to. Joshua worked at Farley's trading post three days a week, walking the five miles in good weather and getting rides when the snow was too deep. He came home in the evenings with stories about the customers — the new settlers coming into the valley, the ranchers expanding their operations, the slow transformation of empty range into something that might eventually become a community.

"Fella came into the post today," Joshua told Hank one Sunday evening. "Said he's bringin' three hundred head up from Texas in the spring. Three hundred. That's twice what Thamon's got. This valley's gonna be crawlin' with cattle by next year."

"And cowboys," Hank said.

"And cowboys," Joshua agreed. "And trouble. More

cattle means more men means more arguments about range and water and whose steer is whose. It's comin', Hank. The territory's changin'."

Hank knew exactly how it was changing. The cattle boom of the 1870s was just beginning. Within a decade, Wyoming would be overrun with ranchers — big operations backed by Eastern and British money, running tens of thousands of head on public range. The tensions between big ranchers and small homesteaders would build for twenty years until they exploded in the Johnson County War of 1892.

He knew all of it. And he couldn't say a word.

Spring came in April — late, grudging, the snow retreating up the mountains an inch at a time like an army that didn't want to surrender. The first green grass appeared along the creek bottoms, and Thamon's surviving cattle found it with the desperate gratitude of animals that had been eating hay and dead grass for four months.

Calving season hit in late April. The busiest, most exhausting, most rewarding time on any cattle ranch — the weeks when the next generation arrived and every hand worked around the clock to make sure the mothers were healthy and the calves were breathing and the predators were kept at bay.

Hank worked calving the way Chester had taught him.

He knew the signs — the restlessness, the separation from the herd, the way a cow's bag filled before delivery. He knew when to intervene and when to let nature handle it. He pulled three calves that were stuck — breech presentations, the calf coming backward, the mother straining and failing. He reached in with hands that had done this a dozen times on Chester's ranch and guided the calves out the way his father had shown him, patient and steady, talking to the mothers in a low voice that calmed them enough to let him work.

Thamon watched him pull the third calf — a big bull that came out backward and sideways and fought every inch of the way — and shook his head in something that looked like wonder.

"You're seventeen years old," Thamon said. "And you handle a calving like a man with thirty years of experience."

"I've been doing this since I was nine," Hank said. The truest thing he'd ever said.

May came. A year. Twelve months since a boy in a jumpsuit and sneakers had fallen out of the sky and landed in a meadow along Clear Creek, confused and terrified and 154 years from home.

Hank stood on the porch of the cabin on a Sunday

morning in May and looked at the valley. The Bighorns were still snow-capped, but the foothills were green and the creek was running high with snowmelt and the grass on the range was thick and new. Thamon's herd — reduced by winter but strengthened by calving — was spread across the south section, grazing on the rotation's freshest pasture.

Everything was alive. Everything was growing. The world was doing what it always did in May — starting over.

A year ago, Hank had been a boy. A seventeen-year-old kid who wore cowboy boots and a straw Resistol and jumped out of planes and helped his father with sixty-five head of cattle and ate his mother's cooking every night at a kitchen table in Buffalo, Wyoming.

He was still seventeen. His birthday — if it had passed, and he thought it had — didn't count in a century that didn't know he existed. But the boy who'd jumped out of that Cessna was gone. In his place stood someone different. Leaner. Harder. His hands were calloused from rope and reins and axe handles. His shoulders were broader from months of lifting logs and hauling hay and wrestling cattle. His face was weathered — not old, but seasoned, the tan and the wind-lines of a man who lived outside in every kind of weather.

And inside, where the changes didn't show, he was different too. He'd built a cabin. He'd saved a herd from disease. He'd survived a Wyoming winter. He'd been in a gunfight and come out alive. He'd sat with a friend who'd been shot and nursed him through a fever. He'd faced a man who wanted to hurt him and hadn't flinched. He'd carried a rock in his chest — Joshua's rock, the one that came from pulling a trigger — and learned to walk with it.

He'd grown up. Not the way you grow up in 2024 — gradually, comfortably, with milestones marked by birthdays and grades and driver's licenses. He'd grown up the way men grew up in 1870 — all at once, under pressure, with the territory itself as the forge and the work as the hammer and the result either something strong or something broken.

Hank wasn't broken. He was strong. Stronger than he'd ever been. Strong enough to carry the weight of two lives — the one he'd lost and the one he'd built.

He looked at the Bighorns. The same mountains his father saw every morning from the ranch in 2024. The same peaks that had watched over this valley since before people existed. They didn't care about centuries or time travel or a boy who'd fallen through a hole in the sky. They just stood there, enormous and patient, the one constant in a world that had changed completely beneath them.

"Mornin'," Joshua said. He came out onto the porch with two cups of coffee, moving slowly because his knees were bad in the mornings but moving with purpose because

Joshua Bettington had stopped waiting to die and started living again. He handed Hank a cup and sat down in his chair.

"Mornin'," Hank said.

"A year," Joshua said. He didn't need to explain. He knew the calendar as well as Hank did — the anniversary of the strange boy who'd fallen out of the sky in bedsheet clothes and funny shoes and turned an old hermit's life upside down.

"A year," Hank said.

"Hell of a year," Joshua said.

"Hell of a year," Hank agreed.

They drank their coffee and watched the morning light move across the valley. The creek ran silver. The cattle grazed. The Bighorns stood above it all, white and blue and permanent.

"Any regrets?" Joshua asked.

Hank thought about it. The honest answer — the answer that lived in the deepest part of him, underneath the rock and the nightmares and the homesickness that had softened but never disappeared — was complicated.

"I miss my family," Hank said. "Every day. I miss my mom and my dad and my brothers. I miss my home. And if someone told me right now that I could go back — step through a door and be in my kitchen in 2024 — I'd go. Without hesitating."

"But?" Joshua said. He heard the word before Hank said it.

"But if I went back," Hank said, "I'd miss you. And Jim. And Thamon. And this cabin and this creek and this valley. I'd miss the life I built here. The person I became here." He looked at Joshua. "You told me once that I was the son you never had. You're the father I found when I lost mine. And this —" He gestured at the cabin, the porch, the mountains, the world. "This is home. Not instead of my real home. Alongside it. Two homes, 154 years apart."

Joshua sipped his coffee. His eyes were bright. "That's the best thing anybody's ever said to me," Joshua said. "And I've been alive sixty-four years, so that's sayin' somethin'."

"It's the truth," Hank said.

"I know it is," Joshua said. "That's why it's the best."

They sat on the porch. A year old, this friendship. A year of beans and coffee and hard work and harder conversations. A year of one boot in front of the other.

The morning was warm. May in Wyoming. The beginning of everything.

Again.

CHAPTER 16: Peace

May settled into the valley the way it always did — slowly, gently, the winter retreating up the Bighorns one day at a time until the snow was just a white line along the highest ridges and the rest of the world was green again.

Hank had a routine now. Not the desperate routine of a boy trying to survive in the wrong century, but the easy, practiced routine of a man who belonged where he was.

Monday through Saturday, he was at Thamon's ranch before dawn. He'd ride Smoke from the cabin in the dark, the .44 on his hip, the Bighorns invisible to the west, the first light catching the creek as he crossed it. He'd work the range all day — checking cattle, riding fence lines that Thamon had started building in the spring at Hank's suggestion, moving the herd between rotation sections, training the two new hands Thamon had hired in April to replace Claven and expand the operation.

The new hands were young — a kid named Virgil Tate from Nebraska, barely eighteen, and a former soldier named Loomis Phelps who'd mustered out of the Army at Fort Fetterman and decided he'd rather chase cattle than Indians. Neither one knew much about ranching, and Thamon had put Hank in charge of teaching them.

"You're my foreman," Thamon had said. Not a question. A fact. The seventeen-year-old who'd arrived a year ago in strange clothes with no horse and no history was now running the daily operations of the largest ranch in the valley. Dollar seventy-five a day, plus the authority to make decisions on the range without checking with Thamon first.

"I'm seventeen," Hank had said.

"And you know more about cattle than any man in this territory," Thamon had said. "Age doesn't matter out here. Competence does."

Hank taught Virgil and Loomis the way Chester had taught him — by doing, by showing, by letting them make small mistakes so they'd avoid the big ones. He showed them how to read cattle — the signs of illness, the patterns of grazing, the subtle behaviors that told you a cow was about to calve or a steer was about to bolt. He showed them the rotation system, the hay-stacking method, the way to manage water sources so the creek banks didn't erode. He showed them everything Chester had put into him, passed down now to two men who would use it to build the cattle industry that would define Wyoming for the next century.

The chain. Joshua's word for it. Somebody helps you, you help somebody else. Pete Sweeney to Joshua. Joshua to Hank. Chester to Hank. Hank to Virgil and Loomis. The knowledge flowing forward through people who cared enough to pass it on.

Jim was riding full days again. The limp was part of him now — as permanent as the scar on his leg where the ball had entered and the slightly crooked way his left boot met the stirrup. He didn't complain about it. Didn't mention it unless someone asked. He just rode and worked and saved his wages and talked about the day when he'd have his own herd.

"Twenty head by next spring," Jim told Hank one afternoon as they rode the north section together. "Thamon's selling me yearlings at a fair price. I've got a spot picked out — six miles north, good water, good grass. I'll run them on open range alongside Thamon's herd until I can build up enough to go independent."

"You'll get there," Hank said.

"I'm already there," Jim said. "In my head, I've been there since the day I left Missouri. The rest is just catching up."

Jim Cotton, Hank thought. Twenty years old, shot in the leg, permanent limp, saving every dollar for a dream he'd been carrying since before he came west. In 2024, Hank would read about men like Jim in history books — the young cowboys who came to Wyoming with nothing and built something from the ground up. Now he was watching it happen in real time, riding beside it, part of the story that would become history.

Sundays were for Joshua.

The cabin on the creek had become the center of Hank's life — not just a place to sleep, but a home. His room had the bed he'd built, a shelf for his few possessions, the canvas sack with his 2024 gear hidden under the floorboards, and a nail on the wall where he hung his hat every night. Joshua's room was across the main space — the Bible on his bedside table, the wool blanket from his old shack that he refused to replace because it was the one thing he'd had when he had nothing.

They had a Sunday routine. Coffee on the porch at dawn. Breakfast — beans and biscuits, still Joshua's specialty, though Hank had taught the old man to make eggs and bacon — eggs from Joshua's chickens that they'd moved to the new cabin, and bacon when they could get it from Farley's post. Then chores — firewood, the chicken coop, the small garden they'd started along the creek where Hank was growing beans and squash using techniques Chester had taught him that were 154 years ahead of anything the local settlers were doing.

After chores, they'd sit. On the porch, in the chairs Hank had built, watching the valley do what it did every day — exist, quietly, beautifully, without needing anything from the men who watched it.

Joshua was sixty-five now. His birthday had passed sometime in the winter — Joshua wasn't sure of the exact date, which was common for men of his generation. "Sometime in January," he'd said. "My mama told me it was cold, but in Colorado it's always cold in January, so that don't narrow it down much."

He looked better than he had a year ago. Not younger — you couldn't reverse sixty-five years of hard living with a cabin and a job. But healthier. Stronger in the way that purpose makes a man stronger. His eyes were brighter. His grin was quicker. He walked the five miles to Farley's post three days a week with the steady determination of a man who had somewhere to be and someone expecting him when he got there.

"Farley says I'm the best worker he's ever had," Joshua told Hank one Sunday. "Course, I'm also the only worker he's ever had, so the competition ain't exactly fierce."

"You're the best worker anybody's ever had," Hank said.

"Now yer just buttering an old man," Joshua said. But he smiled. The smile of a man who'd spent sixty-three years hearing nothing good about himself and was still getting used to hearing it now.

On a Tuesday in mid-May, Thamon called Hank to the ranch house after dinner. The rancher was at his table with a ledger book — the record of his operation, the numbers that told the story of a year. Cattle count, expenses, income, losses.

"I want to show you something," Thamon said. He turned the ledger toward Hank. The numbers were written in Thamon's careful hand — not elegant, but precise. "When you came here a year ago, I had a hundred and fifty head. I lost thirteen to winter. But we got every stolen head back from that canyon, and with spring calving, I've gained forty-one new calves. That puts me at a hundred and seventy-eight head. Biggest herd in the valley."

"The rotation helped," Hank said.

"The rotation helped," Thamon agreed. "The hay helped. The calving techniques helped. You helped, Hank. You walked onto this ranch a year ago and you changed everything about how I run cattle. And I'm not too proud to say that without you, I'd have lost this operation last winter."

"You'd have figured it out," Hank said.

"Maybe," Thamon said. "In five years. Ten. Maybe never. What you brought — wherever you brought it from — gave me a decade's worth of knowledge in twelve months." He closed the ledger. "I owe you more than wages. I want you to know that."

"You don't owe me anything," Hank said. "You gave me a job when I had nothing. You gave me a chance. Everything I've built here started with you saying 'I'll give you a week.'"

"Best week I ever invested," Thamon said.

That Sunday, Hank sat on the porch with Joshua and watched the evening come in. The Bighorns were pink with sunset. The creek was high with snowmelt, running fast over the stones that had been there for centuries and would be there for centuries more. The cattle were dark shapes on the distant range — Thamon's growing herd, spread across pastures that were thick with grass from a year of rotation.

Everything was right. Not perfect — nothing in 1870 was perfect. The nightmares still came, though they were whispers now instead of shouts. The homesickness was still there, a dull ache that lived in his chest beside the rock from the canyon. And the .44 still felt heavy sometimes, the weight of consequence that Joshua said would never fully lift.

But the life was right. The work, the people, the land. The routine of dawn rides and range work and Sunday coffee with an old man who snored through walls and grinned through everything else.

"Joshua," Hank said.

"Yeah, son?" Joshua said.

"I think I'm happy," Hank said. He said it with the surprise of someone discovering something they hadn't expected to find. "Not the way I was happy in — before. Not the same kind. But happy. Here. Now. With this."

Joshua sipped his coffee. Looked at the mountains. Took his time.

"That's because you stopped fightin' it," Joshua said. "First few months, you were fightin' everything — the time, the place, the missin'. You were tryin' to be somewhere else while standin' right here. And that's a war nobody wins." He looked at Hank. "But somewhere along the way, you stopped fightin'. You started livin'. And livin' is where the happy is. It ain't in the place or the time. It's in the doin'. The workin' and the buildin' and the bein' with people who matter."

"You matter," Hank said.

"I know I do," Joshua said. "Took me sixty-four years to matter to somebody, but I got there." He grinned. "Better late than never, I reckon."

"I want you to know something," Hank said. "In case — in case anything ever happens. In case I have to leave suddenly, the way I arrived. I want you to know that this year — this year with you, on this creek, in this cabin — has been the most important year of my life. Not because of the cattle or the ranch or anything I've learned about 1870. Because of you. Because you took in a scared kid who fell out of the sky and you gave him a home and a family and a reason to keep going. You're the best man I've ever known, Joshua. Besides my father."

Joshua was quiet for a long time. The creek ran. The evening deepened. The first stars appeared above the Bighorns.

"If you ever do leave," Joshua said, and his voice was rough in the way it got when the feelings were too big for the words, "I want you to know that this year — this year with you — is the reason I'm still alive. Not the cabin. Not the job. You. The son I never had. The boy who fell out of the sky and made an old man's life worth livin' again."

He reached over and put his hand on Hank's arm. The gnarled, sun-darkened hand of a man who'd spent sixty-five years working and fighting and surviving and had finally, in the last year, found the thing that made all of it mean something.

"Whatever happens," Joshua said, "you remember this porch. You remember this creek. You remember me. That's all I ask."

"I'll remember," Hank said. "Every day. For the rest of my life."

"That's enough," Joshua said. "That's more than enough."

They sat on the porch until the stars filled the sky —

the same enormous, impossible Wyoming sky that covered both their centuries, connecting them across 154 years of history with nothing but light.

CHAPTER 17: The Cabin

The last Sunday in May was a good day. Not extraordinary — not the kind of day that announced itself as important or memorable or different from any other. Just a good day. The kind that earned its place in a life by being exactly what it was supposed to be.

Hank had spent the week on the range, working spring roundup. The herd was scattered across the valley — a hundred and seventy-eight head spread over thousands of acres of open range, with forty-one spring calves that needed counting, checking, and in some cases chasing down when they wandered too far from their mothers. It was the busiest time of year on any ranch, and Thamon's operation was bigger now than it had been twelve months ago, which meant more cattle, more ground to cover, and more hours in the saddle.

Virgil and Loomis were coming along. They weren't natural cattlemen the way Jim was — they didn't have the instinct yet, the ability to read an animal's behavior and predict what it would do before it did it. But they worked hard and they listened and they didn't complain, which put them ahead of most hands in the territory. Hank was patient with them the way Chester had been patient with him — correcting mistakes without anger, demonstrating techniques instead of just describing them, letting them learn by doing.

"You're a good teacher," Jim had told him on Friday, watching Hank show Virgil how to approach a cow with a sick calf without spooking her. "Better than most men twice your age."

"I had a good teacher," Hank had said.

"Your daddy again," Jim said. And grinned.

Saturday had been long — ten hours on the range, pushing cattle to the summer rotation pastures, the grass green and thick from a wet spring. Hank had ridden Smoke hard and come back to the bunkhouse sore and tired and satisfied in the way that only a full day of honest work could produce. The kind of tired that Chester came home with every evening — not exhaustion, but completion. The feeling of a day used up properly.

Sunday morning, Hank rode to the cabin. The ride was second nature now — five miles along the creek, Smoke picking his way through the cottonwoods, the Bighorns rising white and blue to the west. The air smelled like May — warm grass, creek water, the faint sweetness of wildflowers blooming along the banks. The same smell that May had in 2024. Some things didn't change with centuries.

Joshua was on the porch with coffee. Always on the porch. Always with coffee. The constants of a man whose life had become predictable in the best possible way.

"Mornin'," Joshua said.

"Mornin'," Hank said.

He unsaddled Smoke and turned him into the small corral beside the cabin where Dolly was already grazing — the old buckskin mare who'd carried Hank to Thamon's ranch on his first day and now lived a life of comfortable retirement that she'd earned through years of slow, opinionated service.

"How's the roundup?" Joshua asked when Hank settled into his chair with a cup of coffee.

"Good," Hank said. "Forty-one calves, all healthy. The rotation pastures are the best I've seen them. Thamon's talking about expanding — maybe buying another fifty head from the new ranchers coming up from Texas."

"Two hundred head," Joshua said. He shook his head slowly. "When I came to this creek three years ago, there wasn't a cow within twenty miles. Now there's hundreds, and more comin' every month. This valley's changin', Hank."

"Everything changes," Hank said. He knew exactly how much the valley would change — the thousands of cattle that would come in the next decade, the fences, the towns, the railroad, the wars. But today, in May of 1871, the valley was still mostly open and mostly wild and mostly beautiful, and Hank was content to sit on a porch and drink coffee and let the future arrive at its own pace.

They did their Sunday chores. Firewood — Hank split a week's worth while Joshua stacked it against the cabin wall. The chicken coop — collecting eggs, cleaning the nesting boxes, patching a spot where a fox had been testing the wire. The garden — the beans were coming up strong, the squash was spreading, and Hank had planted a row of potatoes that Joshua watched with the skepticism of a man who'd never grown anything in his life and wasn't entirely convinced the earth would cooperate.

"Them potatoes ain't gonna do nothin'," Joshua said, studying the small green shoots.

"Give them time," Hank said.

"I've given everything time," Joshua said. "Time don't always deliver."

"These will," Hank said. "My dad grew potatoes every year. Same soil, same method. They always came through."

"Yer daddy grew potatoes," Joshua said. He smiled. "Is there anything that man didn't teach you?"

"How to fall out of the sky and land in 1870," Hank said.

Joshua laughed. The gap-toothed laugh that Hank had come to love the way he loved the sound of the creek and the sight of the Bighorns and the smell of coffee in the morning. The laugh of a man who was alive because a boy had fallen into his life and given him a reason to stay.

In the afternoon, Hank walked to the creek. Not to sit and think — he'd done enough sitting and thinking to last a lifetime. Just to walk. To feel the ground under his boots and the sun on his face and the May air moving through the cottonwoods. The creek was running high with snowmelt, the water clear and cold, tumbling over stones that had been worn smooth by time that made 154 years look like a heartbeat.

He stood on the bank and looked west. The Bighorns rose above the valley — enormous, patient, unchanged since the day he'd landed in the meadow a year ago. The same mountains Chester saw from the ranch in 2024. The same peaks that had watched over this valley since before people existed.

He thought about his family. Not with the sharp grief of the first months or the dull ache of the middle months. With something gentler. A warmth. The kind of missing that lives alongside happiness without poisoning it. He missed Chester and Hazel and Jules and Sanger the way you miss people you love who are far away but safe — the distance hurt, but the love didn't.

He touched the folded letter in his shirt pocket. Still

there. Always there. The words he'd written on a Sunday in July, sitting on a cottonwood trunk with his feet in this same creek. The letter to a family that would never read it.

He didn't need to read it. He knew every word. And the words were still true — he was living, not just surviving. He was the rancher Chester raised him to be, 154 years early. And if he ever found a way back, the first thing he'd do was hug Hazel so hard she dropped whatever she was cooking.

He smiled. Put the letter back in his pocket. Walked back to the cabin.

Joshua made dinner. Beans and biscuits — his specialty, unchanged in a year of Hank's attempts to expand the menu. "Beans and biscuits kept me alive fur sixty-five years," Joshua said whenever Hank suggested variety. "I ain't fixin' to mess with success."

They ate at the table Hank had built — rough timber, sturdy, big enough for two men and their coffee cups and the silence that lived between them like a third person. The silence of people who'd said everything important and were comfortable with what was left.

"Good beans," Hank said.

"They're always good beans," Joshua said. "That's the thing about beans. They don't try to be somethin' they ain't. They're beans. Honest. Reliable. Never let you down."

"You're describing yourself," Hank said.

"I'm describin' beans," Joshua said. "But I appreciate the comparison."

After dinner, they sat on the porch. The evening was warm — warm enough to sit without a coat, which in Wyoming meant the summer was coming and the worst was behind them. The creek ran silver in the last light. The cattle were distant shapes on the range. The sky was doing the thing it did every evening — turning colors that no painter in any century could capture.

"I'm gonna turn in," Joshua said. He stood slowly — the knees, always the knees — and stretched. "These old bones need more sleep than they used to."

"Goodnight, Joshua," Hank said.

"Goodnight, son," Joshua said. He put his hand on Hank's shoulder as he passed — the brief, firm touch that had become their goodnight ritual. The hand of a father on the shoulder of a son. "See you in the mornin'."

"See you in the morning," Hank said.

Joshua went inside. Hank heard the familiar sounds — boots coming off, the cot creaking, the Bible opening and closing the way it did every night when Joshua read a verse before sleeping. Then the lamp went out, and Joshua's room was dark.

Hank sat on the porch for another hour. He didn't think about anything in particular. Just sat. Watched the stars come out — the enormous Wyoming stars that he'd grown to love, the stars that were the same in 1870 and 2024 and every year in between. Listened to the creek. Felt the air cool as the day gave up its warmth to the night.

The .44 was on his hip. The boots were on his feet. The hat was on his head. The letter was in his pocket.

A year. Twelve months. Three hundred and sixty-five days of working and building and learning and hurting and healing and becoming someone he hadn't known he could be.

Locked in. The hat stays with him on the bed. Here's the final fix for Chapter 17. Replace:

He went inside. Set the .44 on the shelf — within reach but not touching, the compromise he'd made with the gun after the canyon. Pulled off his boots and set them beside the bed — right boot first, then left, the reverse of how he put them on. He meant to hang his hat and change his clothes, but the bed was right there and the tired was bone-deep, and he sat down on the edge meaning to rest for just a minute.

He leaned back. Still dressed — shirt, trousers, vest, the folded letter in his shirt pocket where it always was. The cabin was quiet.

He went inside. Set the .44 on the shelf — within reach but not touching, the compromise he'd made with the gun after the canyon. Pulled off his boots and set them beside the bed — right boot first, then left, the reverse of how he put them on. He meant to change his clothes, but the bed was right there and the tired was bone-deep, and he sat down on the edge meaning to rest for just a minute.

He leaned back. Still dressed — shirt, trousers, vest, the folded letter in his shirt pocket where it always was. The hat was beside him on the bed where he'd tossed it. The cabin was quiet.

Through the wall, he could hear Joshua settling in — the cot shifting, the blanket rustling, and then, within minutes, the snoring. The deep, rattling, wonderful snoring of a sixty-five-year-old man who slept like he had nothing in the world to worry about, because for the first time in his life, he didn't.

Hank lay in the dark and listened. To the snoring. To the creek. To the wind in the cottonwoods. To the sound of a world that had become his home.

He was tired. The good kind of tired — the kind that came from a week of work and a day of chores and an evening of beans and coffee and silence on a porch with a man he loved. The kind of tired that pulled you under gently, without struggle, the way a creek current carries a leaf.

His eyes closed. The sounds blurred together —
snoring, creek, wind, the distant low of a cow somewhere on
the range. The sounds of 1870. The sounds of home.

He fell asleep.

The same way he fell asleep every Sunday night. Boots
by the bed. Hat on the nail. Creek outside the window.
Joshua through the wall.

Nothing different. Nothing special. Just a boy who'd
become a man, falling asleep in the home he'd built, in the
life he'd chosen, on a Sunday night in May.

He didn't know it was the last time.

CHAPTER 18: Home

Hank opened his eyes and the ceiling was wrong.

Not rough timber with gaps where the stars showed through. Not the pine planks he'd helped nail to the rafters of Joshua's cabin. Smooth. White. Flat. A ceiling he'd seen every morning for seventeen years but hadn't seen in twelve months.

His straw Resistol was on the hook where he'd hung it the last time he'd been in this room — Friday night, the night before the jump, a lifetime ago.

He looked down at himself. He was wearing clothes that didn't belong in this room. A cotton shirt — hand-stitched, worn soft from washings in creek water. A leather vest. Trousers held up by a belt Joshua had given him. The clothes of 1870. The clothes he'd fallen asleep in on a Sunday night in a cabin on Clear Creek.

The hat was beside him on the bed. Joshua's hat — not the straw Resistol on the hook, but the older, weathered hat that Joshua had given him a year ago when a scared boy in a jumpsuit needed to look like he belonged. Sun-faded, sweat-stained, shaped by a year of wind and work and weather. A hat that had been worn in a century that ended 124 years before this bedroom existed.

He reached into his shirt pocket. The letter was there.

Folded, worn at the creases, the paper soft from months of being carried against his chest. The letter he'd written on a Sunday in July, sitting on a cottonwood trunk by Clear Creek with his feet in the water. The letter to his family that could never be sent.

Except now he was home. And the family was here. And the letter was in his hand.

Hank stood. His body felt wrong in this room — too big, too heavy, too hard. He looked at his hands. Calloused. Rope-burned. The hands of a man who'd spent a year gripping reins and axes and branding irons. Not the hands of a seventeen-year-old who'd jumped out of a plane on Saturday morning.

He walked to the mirror on the back of his bedroom door. The face looking back at him was his — the same eyes, the same jaw, the same dark hair. But different. His hair was longer, past his collar, not the trimmed cut he'd had on Friday. His face was leaner, the cheekbones sharper, a tan that was deeper than any May in Wyoming could produce in two days. His shoulders were broader under the 1870 shirt. His arms were thicker. His whole body had the hard, defined look of someone who'd spent twelve months doing physical work from dawn to dark without a day off.

Two days. He'd been gone two days in this world. Saturday morning to Monday morning. But his body had lived a year.

He heard footsteps downstairs. Fast. Then his mother's voice — not calling, not speaking. Screaming.

"Chester! Chester, come here! He's — I heard him — Chester!"

The bedroom door flew open. Hazel stood in the doorway. She was in her bathrobe, her hair down, her face — the face Hank had been picturing every night for twelve months — showing every emotion a human being could feel at once. Shock. Disbelief. Relief. Terror. Joy. All of it happening behind her eyes in the two seconds it took her to see her son standing in his bedroom in clothes she'd never seen, looking like a man she barely recognized.

"Hank?" Hazel said. The word came out broken. The word of a mother who'd been told to prepare for the worst and was looking at something she couldn't explain.

"Hey, Mom," Hank said.

Hazel crossed the room in three steps and grabbed him. Not a hug — a seizure. The desperate, crushing grip of a woman who'd spent two days believing her son was dead and was now holding him and couldn't let go because letting go meant he might disappear again.

"Where were you?" Hazel said into his shoulder. She was crying — the hard, shaking sobs of relief that sounded nothing like the crying of sadness. "Where were you? We looked everywhere. The police, the search teams, the whole town. Your skydiving friends, they searched the fields, the creek beds, everywhere. Nobody could find you. Nobody —"

"I'm here, Mom," Hank said. "I'm home."

Chester appeared in the doorway. Hank's father — fifty-two, lean, weathered, the man who spoke in short sentences and long silences — stood in the doorframe and looked at his son. His eyes went from Hank's face to his clothes to his hair to his hands to the hat on the bed. Chester Blankenship processed information the way he processed everything — slowly, thoroughly, missing nothing.

"You're wearing different clothes," Chester said.

"Yeah," Hank said.

"Your hair's longer," Chester said.

"Yeah," Hank said.

"You've put on twenty pounds of muscle since Saturday," Chester said.

"Yeah," Hank said.

Chester looked at him for a long time. The silence between them was the silence of two men who communicated in ways that didn't require words — in shared work and quiet mornings and the rhythm of a ranch that they both understood. Chester didn't ask where. He didn't ask how. He just crossed the room and put his arms around his son, and Hank felt his father's hands — calloused the same way Hank's were calloused now, hard from the same kind of work — grip his shoulders and hold.

"Don't ever do that again," Chester said. His voice was rough.

"I didn't do it on purpose," Hank said.

"I know," Chester said. "Don't do it again anyway."

Jules and Sanger came thundering up the stairs. Jules first — twelve years old, loud, his face a mess of tears and confusion and the wild joy of a kid who'd spent two days thinking his brother was gone forever. He crashed into Hank with the full force of a sixty-pound projectile and held on.

"Where did you go?" Jules yelled. "Where did you go? We looked for you! We looked everywhere! I told them you weren't dead! I told them!"

"I wasn't dead, buddy," Hank said. "I was just far away."

Sanger stood in the doorway the way Chester had — watching, assessing, the fifteen-year-old who processed the world carefully before reacting to it. He looked at Hank's clothes. At the hat on the bed. At the hands that were different, the body that was different, the brother who was the same and not the same.

"You look older," Sanger said.

"I feel older," Hank said.

Sanger walked over and hugged him. Not the crashing impact of Jules — a quiet, firm embrace. The hug of a brother who'd stepped up in Hank's absence and done the chores and ridden the range and been strong for everyone and was now, finally, allowed to stop.

"I'm glad you're back," Sanger said.

"Me too," Hank said.

Hazel made breakfast. Of course she did — because Hazel Blankenship handled every crisis in her life by feeding people, and this was the biggest crisis she'd ever faced and therefore required the biggest breakfast. Eggs, bacon, biscuits, coffee. The kitchen table. The whole family.

Hank sat in his chair — the chair that had been empty for two days, the chair that Hazel had probably stared at every meal since Saturday — and ate his mother's cooking for the first time in a year. The eggs were perfect. The bacon was crisp. The biscuits were warm and soft and tasted like childhood and safety and everything he'd been missing for twelve months.

He almost cried. Not from sadness. From the taste of his mother's food after a year of beans and biscuits and beef cooked over a wood stove. The taste of home.

"You need to tell us what happened," Hazel said. She was sitting across from him, watching him eat, her eyes never leaving his face. "The police are coming back this morning. Everyone's been looking for you. We need to know."

"I know," Hank said. "I just — not yet. I need a little time."

"Take the time you need," Chester said. And that was that. Chester had spoken, and in the Blankenship house, Chester's word was the end of the conversation.

The phone rang. Aunt Tammy. Then Aunt Gylness. Then the police. Then the skydiving club. The house filled with calls and visitors and the noise of a community that had spent two days searching for a missing boy and was now trying to understand how he'd appeared in his own bedroom on Monday morning wearing clothes from another century.

Hank told them nothing. Not the police, not the aunts, not the friends. He told them he'd gotten disoriented during the jump, landed far from the zone, wandered, got lost, found his way back. It was a terrible lie and nobody fully believed it — the clothes, the hair, the muscle, none of it matched a story about getting lost for two days. But nobody could prove otherwise, and after the relief of having him home alive, the questions faded to background noise.

He went back to school on Wednesday. Three days to

finals. The last week of his senior year — the week that was supposed to have started the Monday after the jump, the week he'd planned to coast through with his B average and his graduation guaranteed.

He sat in classrooms and looked at textbooks and listened to teachers and felt like a man visiting a country he'd once lived in. Everything was familiar and everything was foreign. The fluorescent lights were too bright. The chairs were too comfortable. The noise — phones buzzing, voices chattering, music leaking from earbuds — was overwhelming after a year of silence broken only by wind and creek water and Joshua's snoring.

His classmates stared. He looked different and they could see it — the hair, the tan, the way he carried himself. Not like a seventeen-year-old senior killing time until graduation. Like a man who'd been somewhere and done something and come back changed in ways nobody could identify.

Travis stopped him in the hall on Thursday. His closest friend. The kid who'd been in the Cessna, who'd watched Hank jump and never come down.

"Dude," Travis said. "What happened to you?"

"I got lost," Hank said.

"For two days," Travis said. "And you came back

looking like you've been working on a ranch for a year."

"Guess I walk a lot when I'm lost," Hank said.

Travis didn't believe him. Nobody did. But Hank didn't care. The truth was too big and too impossible and too precious to share with anyone who wouldn't understand. And there was only one person in the world who would understand.

He found it on a Thursday night. The history book.

He was studying for his Wyoming History final — the last exam before graduation. The textbook was open on his desk, the chapter on early cattle ranching in the territory. He'd read this chapter before — back in April, before the jump, when it was just history. Names and dates and facts about people who'd lived and died a century and a half ago.

Now he read it again.

The development of cattle ranching in the Johnson County region began in the late 1860s and early 1870s, as settlers moved into the area along Clear Creek at the foot of the Bighorn Mountains.

Hank's hands went still on the page.

Among the earliest and most successful ranchers was Herman Thamon, who established one of the first large herds in the region. Thamon was known for innovative grazing methods, including a pasture rotation system that was decades ahead of its time and helped preserve rangeland that other operations had overgrazed. His ranch grew from modest beginnings to become one of the largest in Johnson County by the late 1870s.

Hank read the words three times. Innovative grazing methods. Pasture rotation system. Decades ahead of its time. His methods. Chester's methods. The knowledge Hank had brought from 2024 and given to a rancher in 1870, written into a history book that Hank was reading 154 years later.

He turned the page.

James "Jim" Cotton was another notable figure in the region's early ranching history. Despite a lifelong limp from an injury sustained while defending a herd from cattle thieves in the early 1870s, Cotton built a successful ranching operation north of the Clear Creek settlement. He was known for his fair dealing and his willingness to help newcomers establish themselves in the territory.

Jim. Jim Cotton. The lean kid from Missouri who'd taught Hank to shoot in a dry wash and helped build a cabin on Sundays and given Hank his Remington before the fight at the canyon. The kid with the limp and the grin and the dream of twenty head on open range. He'd done it. He'd built his ranch. He'd become someone the history books remembered.

Hank turned more pages. Looking. Scanning every

name, every reference, every footnote about the early settlers along Clear Creek. And then, in a passage about the trading post that served the scattered homesteads before Buffalo was founded in 1879, he found it.

The Clear Creek trading post, operated by Emmett Farley, served as the commercial and social hub for settlers in the region throughout the 1870s. Local accounts mention Joshua Bettington, a former ranch hand who worked at the post and was known for his colorful stories and his generosity to travelers. Bettington lived on a homestead along Clear Creek until his death in 1889 at the age of eighty-three.

Joshua lived to be eighty-three. Eighteen years after Hank left — eighteen years of the cabin on the creek, the trading post job, the chickens, the garden, the porch where they'd watched the sunset over the Bighorns. Eighteen more years of living. Not waiting to die — living. The way he'd been living when Hank fell asleep on a Sunday night in May and didn't wake up in the same century.

Hank closed the book. His hands were shaking — not the way they'd shaken after the canyon, with fear and guilt. With something bigger. The overwhelming, chest-crushing realization that every moment of the past year had been real. Every bean Joshua cooked. Every calf Hank pulled. Every round he'd fired in the dry wash. Every Sunday on the porch.

Every nightmare and every sunrise and every boot in front of the other.

Real. All of it. Written into the history of a place he'd lived in twice — once in 1870, once in 2024 — separated by 154 years and connected by a creek that ran through both.

He put his face in his hands and cried. Not the quiet tears of the first months in 1870. The deep, shaking sobs of a man who'd carried something enormous for a year and was finally allowed to set it down.

The names were in the book. The people were in the history. Joshua lived to eighty-three. Jim built his ranch. Thamon's methods — Hank's methods, Chester's methods — changed the way cattle were raised in the territory.

It was real. It was all real.

And Hank was the only person in the world who knew it.

The night before graduation, Hank found his mother in the kitchen. It was late — after ten. Chester was in bed. Jules and Sanger were in their rooms. The house was quiet in the way it got quiet at night, the hum of the refrigerator and the tick of the clock on the wall and the sound of a family sleeping.

Hazel was at the table with a cup of tea. Not doing anything — just sitting. The way she'd been sitting a lot since

Hank came home, as if she was afraid that looking away from her family would make them disappear.

"Mom," Hank said. "I need to tell you something."

"Sit down, baby," Hazel said.

Hank sat across from her. The kitchen table. The same table where he'd eaten breakfast the Friday before the jump. The same table where he'd eaten eggs and bacon on Monday morning when he came back. The table that had been empty for two days and full for a year, depending on which century you were counting.

"I'm going to tell you what really happened," Hank said. "And it's not going to make sense. And you're going to think I'm crazy or lying or both. But I need to tell someone, and you're the only person I trust enough."

"Tell me," Hazel said.

Hank told her.

Everything. From the beginning — the jump, the empty sky, the wrong ground. Landing in the meadow. Joshua's shack. The beans and coffee and the old man who said "you're here now, son." The clothes under the floorboards. Thamon's ranch and the week that became a year. Jim Cotton and the Remington and the dry wash. Claven Clower and the smell and the sabotage and the betrayal. The cabin — the logs and the shakes and the glass windows and Joshua's face when he stood in his own house for the first time. The stolen cattle and the box canyon and the fight. The man on the ridge grabbing his shoulder. The nightmares. Joshua's snoring through the wall. The .44 that he'd learned to shoot and hoped to never use and used and carried the weight of ever since. The winter. The hay. Jim's limp. The porch. The creek. The letter.

He pulled the letter from his shirt pocket — the same shirt he'd been wearing when he woke up Monday morning, washed now but still the hand-stitched cotton of 1870. He unfolded it and laid it on the table.

"I wrote this in July," Hank said. "Sitting by Clear Creek. I was writing to you and Dad and Jules and Sanger. I never thought you'd read it."

Hazel picked up the letter. She read it slowly, her lips moving slightly the way they did when she read student essays at the kitchen table. Her eyes moved across the words — the words of a boy who was 154 years from his mother's cooking and thought he'd never taste it again.

When she finished, she set the letter down. She looked at Hank. Her eyes were wet but her face was steady — the face of a woman who'd spent her whole life dealing with things that didn't make sense and had learned to focus on the things that did.

"The hat," Hazel said. "The one on your bed. That's

not yours."

"It was Joshua's," Hank said. "He gave it to me my second day in 1870. I've been wearing it for a year."

"And the clothes you were wearing Monday morning," Hazel said. "The shirt, the vest. Those aren't from any store I know."

"They're from 1870," Hank said. "Hand-stitched. Joshua's old clothes, given to a boy who fell out of the sky in a jumpsuit."

"And your body," Hazel said. "The muscle. The hair. The calluses on your hands."

"A year of ranch work," Hank said. "Dawn to dark, six days a week. Building a cabin, hauling logs, riding range, pulling calves. A year of work that happened in two days."

Hazel was quiet for a long time. The clock ticked. The refrigerator hummed. The house held its breath.

"The history book," Hazel said. "You found their names."

"Herman Thamon," Hank said. "Jim Cotton. Joshua Bettington. All in the book. All real. Thamon built the biggest ranch in the valley using grazing methods that I taught him — methods Dad taught me. Jim built his own ranch despite the limp. And Joshua —" His voice cracked. "Joshua lived to eighty-three. Eighteen years after I left. He lived, Mom. He didn't die in that shack. He lived in the cabin I built for him and worked at the trading post and he lived."

Hazel reached across the table and took her son's hands. The calloused, rope-burned, 1870 hands of a boy who'd lived a year in two days and come home carrying the weight of it.

"I believe you, Henry," Hazel said. "And I'm so proud of the man you've become."

The words broke him. Not the way the canyon had broken him — with violence and smoke and the weight of a gun. Gently. The way a dam breaks when the water has been pressing against it for too long and the structure finally lets go. He put his head on the table and cried, and Hazel held his hands and let him, because mothers know that some things need to come out before anything else can go in.

When the tears stopped, Hazel got up and did what Hazel always did when the world needed putting back together.

She made him something to eat.

Graduation day. Saturday morning. One week and two days since the jump that changed everything. One year and two days, depending on how you counted.

Hank stood in front of the mirror in his bedroom. He was wearing a button-down shirt and slacks — Hazel's requirement for the ceremony. But the boots were on his feet. Not the 1870 boots — his own cowboy boots, the brown leather ones that had been sitting by the bedroom door for a year, waiting for him to come home.

And the hat. Joshua's hat. Not the straw Resistol — that hat belonged to a boy who'd jumped out of a plane and never came all the way down. Joshua's hat belonged to the man who'd landed.

"You're wearing that hat to graduation?" Jules asked from the doorway. "It looks old."

"It is old," Hank said. "Older than you know."

"You're weird," Jules said. "Come on, Mom says we're leaving in ten minutes."

The ceremony was in the high school gymnasium. Sixty-three graduates in caps and gowns, families in the bleachers, the principal at the podium. Hank sat in his alphabetical seat and listened to the speeches and the names and the applause and felt the strangeness of being in two places at once — here, in this gym, in 2024, and there, on a porch on Clear Creek, in 1871, watching the sunset with an old man who considered him a son.

"Henry Blankenship," the principal called.

Hank stood. Walked to the stage. Cowboy boots under the gown. Joshua's hat in his hand — he'd taken it off inside because Hazel had raised him right. The principal shook his hand and gave him the diploma and Hank turned to face the audience.

Chester and Hazel in the front row. Chester's face — steady, proud, the most emotion Hank had ever seen on it. Hazel beside him, crying and smiling at the same time, the way only mothers can. Jules standing on the bleacher seat to see better, yelling something that was probably embarrassing. Sanger sitting quietly, watching his brother the way he watched everything — carefully, completely, with the understanding that some moments were too important for noise.

And Aunt Tammy and Aunt Gylness, side by side, both crying, both talking, probably giving each other advice about how to cry properly at a graduation.

His family. The family he'd missed for a year. The family he'd written a letter to from a creek in 1870. The family he'd come home to.

Hank walked off the stage with his diploma in one hand and Joshua's hat in the other. He walked straight to his mother and hugged her — hard, the way he'd promised in the letter. Hard enough that she gasped.

"I love you, Mom," Hank said.

"I love you too, baby," Hazel said. "Now let me go

before you break me."

He hugged Chester. His father held him the way Chester held everything — steady, firm, saying nothing because nothing needed to be said. Two ranchers. Two men who communicated through work and silence and the shared understanding of what it meant to care for land and animals and family.

"Proud of you," Chester said. Two words. From Chester Blankenship, that was a speech.

"Thanks, Dad," Hank said. "For everything you taught me. You have no idea how much it mattered."

Chester looked at him with an expression that was almost a question. Almost. But Chester didn't ask questions he wasn't sure he wanted answered. He just nodded and clapped his son on the shoulder and let it go.

That evening, after the celebration, after the cake and the aunts and the neighbors and the phone calls, Hank went to his room. He changed out of the graduation clothes and into jeans and a flannel shirt and his cowboy boots. He hung Joshua's hat on the hook beside the straw Resistol. Two hats. Two lives.

He sat on his bed and pulled the letter from where he'd put it — the top drawer of his nightstand, beside the copy of "Lonesome Dove" and the phone he'd learned to live without.

He read it one more time.

Dear Mom and Dad and Jules and Sanger,

I'm okay. I know you can't hear this and I know you don't know where I am and I know that's the worst part. But I'm okay...

He folded the letter and put it back. He'd keep it forever. The way he'd keep Joshua's hat and the calluses on his hands and the memory of a porch on Clear Creek and the sound of an old man snoring through a cabin wall.

He'd keep all of it. Every moment. Every sunrise. Every boot in front of the other.

Because some things — a year in the Old West, an old man's friendship, the weight of a .44 in a shaking hand, the sound of Clear Creek in 1870 — are too real to forget.

Even when nobody else can understand them.

Hank lay back on his bed. His bed. In his room. In his house. In 2024. The ceiling was smooth and white and familiar. The boots were by the door. Two hats hung on the wall. The letter was in the drawer. And through the window, invisible in the dark but there — always there — the Bighorn Mountains rose above Buffalo, Wyoming, the same mountains that had watched over him in both his lives.

He closed his eyes.

For the first time in a year, the dreams that came were not nightmares. They were Sunday mornings on a porch. Coffee in a tin cup. Beans and biscuits. Gap-toothed grins. The sound of a creek running over stones that had been there for centuries and would be there for centuries more.

The sound of home. Both of them.

THE END

Acknowledgments

This book exists because of the people who believed in it before it was finished.

To my readers — thank you for coming back. Every book I write is for you, and every story I tell is better because I know you're out there waiting for it.

To the town of Buffalo, Wyoming, and Johnson County — your history is extraordinary. The ranchers, the settlers, the cowboys, and the Native peoples who shaped this valley deserve to be remembered. I've taken liberties with names and events, but the land is real, the history is real, and the spirit of the place is something I've tried to honor on every page.

To the Jim Gatchell Memorial Museum in Buffalo and the Hoofprints of the Past Museum in Kaycee — thank you for preserving the stories that inspired this novel. If you haven't visited, you should.

To the men and women who built Wyoming's cattle industry from nothing — on open range, in brutal winters, with nothing but horses and rope and stubbornness — this book is a small tribute to what you accomplished.

And to every young person who's ever looked at the sky and wondered what was on the other side — keep jumping.

A Note from the Author

I've been fascinated by the American West my whole life. As a boy, I watched every western movie I could find. As a man, I read the history behind those movies and discovered that the real West was harder, more dangerous, and more remarkable than anything Hollywood ever put on screen.

Hank Blankenship is a fictional character, but the world he lands in is as real as I could make it. In 1870, the area that would become Buffalo, Wyoming, was open range at the foot of the Bighorn Mountains — no town, no law, no fences. Cattle ranching was just beginning. The settlers who came to that valley were building something from nothing, and the risks they took were extraordinary.

The characters Hank meets — Joshua, Herman Thamon, Jim Cotton — are fictional, but they represent the real men and women who built Johnson County. Their methods, their struggles, and their courage are drawn from the historical record.

One thing the research taught me is that the Old West wasn't the romantic adventure the movies made it seem. It was work. Hard, dangerous, unglamorous work. The cowboys who lived it didn't wear clean hats and shiny boots. They wore out their bodies and buried their friends and kept

going because that was the only option the territory gave
them.

Hank learns this lesson the hard way. I hope his story
helps readers appreciate what "the Old West" really meant —
not just the adventure, but the cost.

This is a work of fiction. But the land is real. The
mountains are real. And Clear Creek still runs through
Buffalo, Wyoming, the same way it did in 1870.

About the Author

Jackie L. Smith is a United States Navy veteran and author of fiction spanning thrillers, middle-grade fantasy, young adult historical fiction, and family drama. Drawing on decades of service in the U. S. Navy, hospital administration, and service in the U. S. Air Force as a civilian, he writes stories rooted in duty, loyalty, and the bonds that hold families together — even when those bonds are tested to the breaking point. He holds a Master's degree from Central Michigan University and lives in eastern Kentucky.

Discussion Questions

1. Hank's friends say he should have been born in a prior century. When he actually lands in 1870, the reality is nothing like the romantic version of the West he imagined from movies. How does the gap between the movie West and the real West shape Hank's experience? What does the novel say about the difference between romanticizing the past and living in it?

2. Joshua Bettington takes in a stranger who fell from the sky wearing clothes that don't exist yet, and his response is to offer food and a place to sleep. What does Joshua's reaction tell us about frontier hospitality and about Joshua as a man? How would a stranger in similar circumstances be received today?

3. Hank's knowledge of modern cattle ranching — grazing rotation, disease management, hay storage — gives him an enormous advantage in 1870. Is it fair for Hank to use knowledge from the future without explaining where it comes from? Does the fact that he can't explain the truth justify the deception?

4. Chester Blankenship teaches his sons by doing, not by lecturing. How does Chester's parenting style shape who Hank becomes in 1870? Can you identify specific

moments where Hank draws directly on something Chester taught him?

5. Joshua tells Hank that "a gun ain't a toy and it ain't a friend — it's a tool." How does Hank's relationship with the .44 change over the course of the novel? What does the novel say about the real cost of violence, compared to how violence is portrayed in western movies?

6. Claven Clower is bitter, resentful, and ultimately a traitor. But he's also a man who's been working for three years without recognition while a seventeen-year-old newcomer gets praised and promoted. Does understanding Claven's frustration change how you see him? Is there a point where his resentment becomes something more dangerous than jealousy?

7. When Hank shoots at the man on the ridge and doesn't know whether he hit him, the not-knowing haunts him more than a definite answer would. Why is uncertainty worse than certainty in this situation? How does this connect to Joshua's story about carrying a "rock in the chest" after shooting a man in Colorado?

8. Hank writes a letter to his family that he knows can never be sent. Why does he write it? What does the act of writing — putting words on paper for an

audience that will never read them — do for Hank
emotionally?

9. Hank tells Joshua that 1870 has become his home
"alongside" his real home — not instead of it. Is it
possible to have two homes in two different times?
What does Hank gain in 1870 that he didn't have in
2024, and what does he lose?

10. When Hank finally tells Hazel the truth, she believes
him without question. Why does Hazel believe him?
What evidence — physical, emotional, or otherwise —
convinces her? And why does Hank choose to tell his
mother instead of his father, his brothers, or his
friends?